GAELIC
SPIRIT

Praise for Gerard Siggins' books

'Superbly written … well worth a read …
Perfect for any sports mad youngster'
Irish Mail on Sunday

'brimming with action and mystery'
Children's Books Ireland

'a brilliant read'
Sunday World

GERARD SIGGINS was born in Dublin and has had a lifelong interest in sport. He's lived almost all his life in the shadow of Lansdowne Road; he's been attending rugby and soccer matches there since he was small enough for his dad to lift him over the turnstiles. He has been a journalist for more than thirty years, specialising in sport. His other books about Eoin Madden – *Rugby Spirit*, *Rugby Warrior*, *Rugby Rebel*, *Rugby Flyer*, *Rugby Runner* and *Rugby Heroes* – as well as his 'Sports Academy' series – *Football Fiesta* and *Rugby Redzone*, are also published by The O'Brien Press.

GAELIC
SPIRIT

GERARD SIGGINS

THE O'BRIEN PRESS
DUBLIN

First published 2020 by
The O'Brien Press Ltd,
12 Terenure Road East, Rathgar,
Dublin 6, Ireland
D06 HD27
Tel: +353 1 4923333; Fax: +353 1 4922777
E-mail: books@obrien.ie.
Website: www.obrien.ie
The O'Brien Press is a member of Publishing Ireland.

ISBN: 978-1-78849-185-3

8 7 6 5 4 3 2 1
23 22 21 20

Printed and bound by Norhaven Paperback A/S, Denmark.
The paper in this book is produced using pulp from managed forests.

Published in

DUBLIN

UNESCO
City of Literature

DEDICATION

To the memory of Fiachra Ó Marcaigh, a man who loved words, music, sport, nature, Donegal and his native Dublin. But most of all he loved family and friends – and was much loved in return.

ACKNOWLEDGEMENTS

Gaelic Spirit is the eighth book featuring Eoin Madden and his friends, but the first in which he returns to his first love, Gaelic games. Thanks for his help to Ronan Early, and to Michael Foley whose masterpiece *The Bloodied Field* (O'Brien Press, 2014) was both an inspiration and a guidebook to a tragic day.

Thanks also to Martha, Jack, Lucy and Billy, and Mam and Dad, for all their support. Thanks to everyone at O'Brien Press, especially my amazing editor Helen Carr.

CHAPTER 1

'Summer holidays are never long enough,' sighed Alan. 'By the time you've wound down from a hard year of schoolwork and exams, done a couple of summer camps and gone on holidays with the family, there's not a lot of time left for real fun.'

'You're right,' said Eoin, 'but you can be a bit clever about it. Skip the summer camps, tell your parents you'd prefer to see a bit more of Ireland, and come down here instead. We've loads of room and there's plenty of crack we can get up to.'

Alan stretched out on the duvet and dropped his mobile on the floor. He scrambled to retrieve it from the scattering of dirty socks under his bed.

'Sorry about that, Eoin,' he started. 'I think I cracked the screen too!'

His pal made sympathetic noises from 150 kilometres away in Ormondstown, the County Tipperary town where he lived with his mum and dad when he wasn't at boarding school in Dublin.

'Do you think your folks would let you come down to stay?' Eoin asked.

'I'd say they'd love that,' Alan replied. 'Dad was complaining last night that it was so expensive for us all to fly to this place Mum wants to go. I told him I was worried about my carbon footprint and would prefer to go somewhere less damaging to the environment.'

'And what did they say to that?' asked Eoin.

'Well, they looked at me a bit funny, but Dad said I made a fair point. I'd say if I told him I could stay in Ireland and save the cost of my flights he'd be delighted.'

'Go for it,' said Eoin. 'Mam is always telling me to invite you down again. You're the only one that eats her apple tarts without making faces so she's a huge fan.'

'Ah lovely, I can taste them now,' Alan chuckled. 'Tell her I'll give her a bit of notice of my arrival so she can start baking.'

'Go on, you cheeky pup, drop me a text later when you know what's happening. I'm playing a bit of hurling this summer so I'd better get moving or I'll be late for training.'

Eoin pressed the red 'off' button and swung his legs out of bed. His summer holiday had started a bit later than Alan's, thanks to his selection for the British and Irish Lion Cubs rugby tour of New Zealand. As he dressed, he thought back to that amazing trip, which had passed so quickly.

He debated wearing the famous red rugby jersey to training, but didn't want to appear too much of a show-off, so he slipped on the equally magical blue and yellow hurling shirt of his native county. There'd be a few lads wearing that, but it was also a present from his grandfather, Dixie Madden, and that made it even more special.

Eoin's dad had already left for work so his mother was reading the newspaper when he walked into the kitchen.

She gave him her usual smile, which turned into a huge grin when he told her he was thinking of inviting Alan down for a few weeks.

'That would be fantastic,' she said. 'It would be great for you to have a bit of extra company around the house, and he's such a lovely polite boy.'

After breakfast, Eoin asked were there any chores she needed him to do before he headed down to the club, but she waved him away.

'No, run along there and do your training. I'd better start peeling some apples, I've got a few tarts to make.'

CHAPTER 2

Eoin tapped his hurley on Dylan's door with a rat-a-tat-tat. It took a minute or two, and when it was finally answered it was Dylan's sister Caoimhe who did so.

'Hiya, Ki,' Eoin grinned. 'Dylan having another lie on?'

'Ah, you know what he's like Eoin, he's been up all night playing his X-Box.'

'I was not,' came a voice, growling as he stumbled down the stairs. 'I switched it off at two o'clock.'

'Yeah, and then you woke me up going downstairs for a drink of water,' replied his sister.

'How are you fixed for a bit of hurling?' asked Eoin, checking the time on his phone. 'We're starting in ten minutes.'

'I'll be with you in two,' said Dylan, backing up the stairs at pace.

'So how was New Zealand?' asked Caoimhe.

'It was great,' replied Eoin. 'But an awful long way to go for three or four matches. The jetlag had me flattened for days.'

'I wish I could get jetlag,' sighed Caoimhe. 'I haven't been on a plane for years. Mam says she can't afford a summer holiday this year either.'

Eoin looked at the ground, a bit embarrassed that he had complained about the long flights.

'Sorry to hear that,' he said, 'maybe things will come around a bit for her.'

'I wish I was allowed to work,' said Caoimhe, 'I'd love to help her out. She's doing two jobs, but never seems to have enough money.'

Dylan charged down the stairs carrying his hurley and helmet.

'Come on, Eoin, let's get down there. Are you playing camogie today, Ki?'

His sister shook her head. 'No, the coach has left, he's got a job in London. They're trying to get someone sorted for the weekend.'

The boys raced down to the Ormondstown Gaels' field where about twenty of their friends were already gathered. Paddy, their coach, was organising them into small groups as they trotted onto the field.

'Sorry, Paddy, I slept it out,' called Dylan.

'Hurry on there, you two,' answered Paddy with a growl.

The old groundsman, Barney, chuckled as he steered his pitch-marking device along the sideline.

'You'd be late for your own funeral,' he called out to Dylan, who responded with a friendly wave.

Paddy despatched Eoin and Dylan to different groups and, after some stretching and warming up, set them on various drills such as contesting the sliotar on the ground and in the air.

Eoin found it tricky to adapt his approach from having played rugby for almost a full year. He had to fight the urge to tackle his opponent around the waist and drag him to the ground.

He settled in quickly, though, and loved the feeling of smacking a sliotar straight and true between the posts, just like a well-struck conversion.

The session flew by, and Paddy divided them into two teams for a ten minutes each way match. Eoin enjoyed the competitive side of it and was thrilled to make the pass through to Isaac who nailed the winning point.

'Good work, lads,' said Paddy. 'I hope you're all around

at the weekend? We've been invited down to Clonmel for a couple of challenge matches, football and hurling. The chairman's brother lives down there and he's keen to get a bit of a thing going between the clubs.'

There was a buzz among the boys – everyone loved away games, especially one that involved an 80km bus journey to the other end of the county.

Every one of the players put their hand up.

'Great stuff, so be here at nine o'clock on Saturday, and bring five euro for the bus. And money for your lunch too.'

Dylan took his hand down.

'Sorry, Paddy, I forgot we've a Mass to go to over in Roscrea. I won't be available.'

CHAPTER 3

Eoin still had a little money in his piggy bank left over from the tour to New Zealand. He emptied it out and saw he had enough to cover the trip to Clonmel as well as a few bars and snacks for the journey. He'd have to get a few paying chores to replenish his coffers – or he and Alan would have a boring few weeks.

'Do you want me to cut the grass, Mam?' he called down to his mother.

'You cut it two days ago,' she replied. 'Even you don't need a haircut that often.'

Eoin grinned. 'Oh yes, I forgot. It's just that…'

'…You're looking for a few bob to supplement your pocket money, is it?' she said. 'Well, I'm pretty much sorted out here. Why don't you go down and see if Dixie needs a hand doing any heavy lifting or chopping in his garden?'

Eoin grabbed his jacket. 'Thanks, Mam, great idea. I'd

love a go of his chainsaw.'

'Don't you dare go near that,' called out his mother. 'Or the heavy axe either.'

Her son grinned, knowing well that Dixie, his grandfather, wouldn't let him use anything so dangerous. He made the journey to Dixie's home on the other side of Ormondstown in less than ten minutes, including three brief stops to receive the congratulations of neighbours or former school friends.

'You were a big star down in New Zealand,' said one old lady. 'Your grandfather was very proud of you. He told me every single day how you were getting on.'

Eoin blushed, thanked the old lady, and ran the last two hundred metres to Dixie's cottage as fast as he could. When he arrived his grandfather was leaning on the gate watching the world go by.

'Ah young Eoin, where are you rushing to on a lovely day like this?' he asked.

'To see you, Grandad!' Eoin replied, his chest heaving as he tried to catch his breath.

'And where's the hurry in that,' he smiled. 'Sure I'll be here all day.'

'I know that, it's just I was wondering if you needed a hand with anything in the garden. Or the house. Or run you a few messages?'

'Well, that's good to hear that you're mad for a bit of work,' answered his grandfather. 'Or are you just mad for a bit of pocket money?'

Eoin laughed. 'Ah, Grandad, you know I'd do your messages for nothing at all. You're always buying me cool rugby shirts and the like.'

'And hurling shirts too,' Dixie replied. 'We're the All-Ireland champions down here now, and let's not forget to remind the rest of them of that.'

'I wore it down to practice earlier,' said Eoin. 'We've a game on down in Clonmel on Saturday. I'm trying to raise the price of the bus ticket. It's a fiver.'

'I'm sure I can stump up that for a reasonable amount of digging out the back. I've a plan to start a vegetable patch. Would your pal Dylan like a job too?' he asked.

'That's a great idea, Grandad,' said Eoin. 'His mam doesn't get paid much in work and they're struggling to get by – I think he'd be glad of the money.'

'Well I'm happy to help out – but I'll want good work for it too.'

Eoin texted his pal to tell him of Dixie's offer, and he got a quick reply.

'Ys plz. Der in 5,' came the text.

'He'll be here in five minutes,' explained Eoin.

'How can you work that out?' asked Dixie. 'It looks

like Hungarian to me.'

Eoin laughed and began explaining the message, but Dixie brushed him off.

'No, no, no. I'm too old to learn another language. I've been picking up some Chinese from the girls down in the supermarket and that's enough new stuff for me.'

'Chinese, eh? So, show me' he asked.

'OK,' replied Dixie. '*Ni hao,*' he added, with a grin.

'And what does that mean?'

'Eh, it means "hello",' replied Dixie.

'Great, and what else did you learn?'

'*Xie, xie* – that's "thank you".'

'And…'

'Nothing else – but sure that's all I'd really need to say, I suppose.'

Eoin laughed, and was still chuckling when Dylan arrived at the gate a few seconds later.

'Howya Dixie,' he grinned. 'I hear you need a strong fella to do a bit of work because this lad isn't quite up to it?'

Eoin flicked his baseball cap at Dylan who ducked, leaving the cap to fly harmlessly into the road where it landed in a puddle.

'Ah now, look at what you made me do!' moaned Eoin.

'See what I mean Dixie,' said Dylan. 'He'd probably cut the heads off the wrong flowers too.'

CHAPTER 4

With Dylan around, the time spent working digging Dixie's back garden passed quickly. The old man kept them well refreshed with orange squash and chocolate biscuits, and they finally cleared the patch as the church bell across the road sounded six o'clock.

'Well, that's enough for today,' called Dixie, as he examined the ground and bent to pick up a weed. 'Come in and wash your hands and I'll settle up with you.'

The boys rinsed their hands under the running tap in the kitchen and wiped them on their jeans.

Dixie came back in clutching two ten-euro notes.

'You worked well today lads so I've decided to give you a bonus. You'll need a bit extra for a long journey to Clonmel anyway.'

Eoin grinned widely and thanked the old man.

'That's very sound of you, Dixie,' said Dylan, 'but I should probably get a bit more than Eoin because I completely showed him up out there with the digging. Let's call it twelve and eight, will we?' he said, winking at the old man.

Eoin's grandfather looked at him and grinned too.

'I think you need to work out these details in advance Dylan. Maybe Eoin ought to get more because he organised the job and then hired you as a sub-contractor?'

Both boys looked stunned for a second or two, before Dixie erupted in laughter.

'Here, take one each and stop your squabbling. You're both excellent workers and once I get this place sorted there'll be plenty of work for you in the garden.'

He looked at the mucky mess that had gathered in his sink and sighed.

'It's a pity you're not a bit more useful around the house. I could do with a hand with these chores. I'm just too tired to keep the house tidy anymore.'

Eoin and Dylan strolled down the town together with their newly earned banknotes in their pockets.

'It's a shame you have that Mass in Roscrea,' said Eoin.

Dylan looked confused for a second, before saying 'Oh that, yeah I think it might have been postponed for a week. I can go now. I better text Paddy.'

'But how did you find that out?' asked Eoin, puzzled. 'Sure, you haven't seen your mam since training.'

Dylan looked away, and just at that moment spotted a gang of older boys coming down the street towards them.

'Hey Eoin, I think we should scarper. These lads look a bit rough and we've worked too hard for our wages to lose them to that crowd.'

Dylan checked the traffic and scooted across the road, followed by Eoin. As soon as they reached the other footpath they broke into a sprint and didn't stop until they reached the chip shop.

'What was that about?' gasped Eoin as he fought to recapture his breath.

'That's Rocky Ryan and his gang. They're a few years ahead of Caoimhe in school. They're always cornering smaller kids and nicking their lunch money.'

'They'd have hit the jackpot with us. Great thinking Dyl,' replied Eoin.

As they chatted outside the chipper, along came another of their team-mates, Isaac.

'Are ye alright there, lads?' he asked, as they recovered from their unscheduled sprint.

While Dylan explained what had happened, Isaac winced.

'I know Rocky and his gang well. They seem to have a problem with me and my brother and the colour of our skin,' he replied, with a frown. 'They say horrible things to us.'

'Really?' said Eoin. 'That's shocking – you need to tell the teachers that.'

'And what would happen then?' replied Isaac. 'We'd just get another beating from Rocky.'

'That's brutal,' agreed Dylan. 'Stick with us, Isaac, he wouldn't do anything to you when I'm around.'

Eoin laughed. 'Sure, you were the first to run as fast as you could at the very sight of him!'

CHAPTER 5

The night before the trip to Clonmel, Eoin found it hard to sleep. He realised he hadn't played a Gaelic football or hurling match for almost two years and he had played so much rugby in between he was afraid he might do something stupid.

He thought back to his very first rugby match and how he had mixed it up with Gaelic football – the other way around – and he smiled.

He was also a bit excited to visit Clonmel, as one of his very best friends since he had moved to boarding school in Dublin four years before was a man from that town.

Well, not really a man. More of a ghost.

Brian Hanrahan was his name, and about a hundred years ago he was a really good rugby player with the Lansdowne club. But he was badly injured in a match at Lansdowne Road and passed away from his injuries.

Eoin had bumped into Brian's ghost on a school visit to Aviva Stadium and they became great friends. Eoin remembered how Brian had helped him settle into playing rugby and his advice was useful in turning him into the excellent player he had become.

Brian had been with him for almost all his adventures, but they had last met months before at Croke Park, when Eoin went to see Ireland play a big game there after the Aviva Stadium was closed down for repairs.

'I wonder does he ever visit Clonmel,' thought Eoin. 'From what he told me, all of his family left there a long time ago.'

Next morning, Eoin's dad called him early and had a big plate of sausages, eggs and bacon ready on the kitchen table.

'Good morning, Dad, that's excellent,' Eoin greeted him with a grin. 'That will set me up perfectly for the journey – if not for the match.'

'Well, Dixie always swore by having a good breakfast on the morning of a game. I'm sure he'd approve of that. Make sure you drop in to see him on the way down to the Gaels.'

Eoin set off a few minutes early to allow for the stops

along the way – his grandfather was carrying a mop and seemed a bit grumpy, but he slipped Eoin a couple of chocolate biscuit bars.

'One for Dylan, now, don't forget,' he grinned, as he waved off his grandson.

The next stop was his pal's house, where Dylan's mum opened the door.

'Good morning, Mrs Coonan,' Eoin said.

'Good morning, Eoin, great to see you back from your travels. I've been shouting for that Dylan for half an hour, I hope he's up and dressed.'

Eoin checked the time on his phone. 'We've a bit of time to spare yet, but we'll need to leave here in the next ten minutes,' he said.

Dylan's mum ran up the stairs and knocked on her son's door before entering his bedroom.

'Dylan!' she called, hammering loud enough for Eoin to hear downstairs.

'Oh no,' came the reply, 'what time is it?'

'You've to be down the club in fifteen minutes. I can drop you down, but you need to get dressed immediately.'

She wandered back downstairs, shrugging her shoulders at Eoin.

'He's a great kid, but he's very hard to shift out of bed.

I heard ye were working over in Dixie's yesterday?'

Eoin nodded. 'Yeah, I think we've got the job as his official gardeners.'

'Ah, he's a lovely man, and very generous.'

'He's always been very good, I'm his only grandkid so he spoils me. But we certainly earned our tenner yesterday.'

'Tenner?' asked Mrs Coonan, just as Dylan charged down the stairs.

'Is there any breakfast? Anything I can eat on the run?' he asked.

His mum shrugged and went to the kitchen to make him a sandwich while Dylan packed his kitbag. He ushered Eoin outside to the car.

'Did I hear you tell her how much we got?' he whispered.

Eoin nodded.

'OK, just don't talk about it again in front of her, right?' he urged.

Dylan's mum came out and handed him a packet of sandwiches wrapped in tin foil.

'Have you enough there – I made an extra one in case you're hungry. They'll give you lunch down there I presume.'

Eoin started to answer her, but something told him it

was better to say nothing. Dylan made eye contact but didn't reply.

The journey to Ormondstown Gaels was quick and Eoin felt a shiver of excitement as he saw the bus parked outside the dressing rooms.

'Hurry on there, Dylan,' called Paddy. 'Ye're the last two. As usual!'

Dylan laughed and climbed the steps, pausing to call out his thanks to his mother and wave her goodbye.

CHAPTER 6

When everyone was aboard the bus, the driver closed the doors and Paddy stood up.

'Quiet down the back,' he started. 'I hope you all had a good night's sleep and a healthy breakfast?'

'We won't be stopping on the road to Clonmel so I don't want anyone singing "Stop the bus I want a wee wee",' he added, which got a good laugh.

'The journey will take about an hour and a half so settle down and don't eat all your sweets before the game. And no fizzy drinks either.'

There was plenty of room on the bus so Eoin got to stretch out across two seats. He checked his phone and found a text from Alan.

'Hey legend. I'm on bus 2 O-town. In @ 11. Can you collect me?'

Eoin replied, explaining that he wouldn't be there, but would ask his parents to meet Alan off the bus.

'On way 2 Clonmel 4 hurling match. C U l8r.'

He texted his mother and she agreed to collect Alan, so Eoin put away the phone and closed his eyes.

He hadn't been used to the early start so hoped to catch up on his sleep. That was a hope doomed to fail as Dylan squeezed in beside him. He didn't look happy.

'What did you go and tell Mam about the tenner for?' he asked.

'It just slipped out, I didn't think it was a big deal. And why IS it a big deal?'

Dylan looked at the back of his hands, and out the window, before replying.

'Well, it's like this,' he started. 'Mam doesn't get much money from the job she does, so I decided to give her half of my pay from Dixie.

'She went mad and refused to take it, saying I had earned it. So I told her Dixie gave us twenty each and I only needed a fiver for the bus, and that I had plenty for myself.

'She was happy enough with that, but if she thinks she took all my spare cash she'll be upset.'

Eoin winced, and apologised. 'I didn't realise that, mate, sorry.'

'Ah I suppose you weren't to know,' Dylan replied.

Eoin remembered that Dylan had originally pulled

out of the bus trip once Paddy mentioned it would cost five euro.

'So, there was no Mass in Roscrea either?'

Dylan nodded.

'Don't worry, mate. And if you're ever stuck don't worry about asking me for a loan. They gave us pocket money every week in New Zealand, but living in the hotels we couldn't really spend it.'

'Nice one,' said Dylan, 'but I think I'll go looking for more work around the town. I think I could get the hang of that gardening. I might even hire you as my labourer – on a smaller wage, of course,' he grinned.

Isaac popped his head between the seats behind.

'I couldn't help hearing what you said and I hope you've room for an assistant labourer? There's a shed at the back of where we're staying and it's full of old gardening tools belonging to the old lad that used to live there. He's in a nursing home now and no one bothered to collect them so I'm sure it would be OK to use them.'

'That's great, Isaac, why don't we start looking for customers on Monday. We'll go around all the houses that look like the garden might need tidying up.'

'Sounds like I've been sacked, eh?' laughed Eoin.

'Well, Isaac is bringing some tools and machinery to the business, what are you bringing?' asked Dylan.

'I got you your first client, for a start,' he replied. 'But don't worry about it – Alan's arriving this morning so I won't have much time for work. We're available to give you a hand at the big jobs though.'

'Alan? I doubt he'd be up for much work,' chuckled Dylan. 'But yeah, that would be handy.'

The journey sped by and they soon reached the ground of their opponents.

'Right lads,' announced Paddy from the front of the bus as the driver parked it behind the clubhouse.

'Get out and stretch yourselves and then go and tog out,' he went on. 'We'll get a bit of a run in before we start. We're playing football first and then hurling. There's twenty-seven here so everyone will start in one or the other. A couple of you will have to start both, but we'll take you off for a rest.

'Now, out you go and remember – you're representing the Gaels.'

CHAPTER 7

Eoin and Dylan rambled into the dressing room and quickly changed into their gear. Paddy arrived with a huge sack and tossed them each a maroon Ormondstown Gaels jersey.

'Now I know we haven't played football much this summer, but you all know your way around so I'll leave you in roughly the same positions as you play in hurling. Here's your jersey, Isaac,' he added, handing him the bright yellow goalkeeper's shirt.

'Eoin, you're new to the team, but I was reading how you play out-half and you're a big kicker,' Paddy began. 'So we'll stick you at centre-field, and maybe push you up on to the half-forward line after a while.'

Eoin nodded, happy to get any sort of role, but a little nervous now that he had been handed such an important one.

He pulled the number nine shirt over his head and

stood up.

'Come on, Dylan, you're such a snail,' he said to his pal, who was still struggling to get his second sock on.

Eoin wandered out onto the field and did a few jumps and stretches to get himself going. Paddy was still urging the stragglers out onto to the field so Eoin started to jog towards the goal at the far end of the ground.

As he neared the nets, he noticed a familiar figure walking through the hedge that acted as a boundary to the club. He was wearing a black, red and yellow jersey that he recognised as that of Lansdowne rugby club, although in a style that hadn't been seen since the late 1920s.

'Brian!' he called out, delighted to see his old pal once again.

'Good morning, Eoin,' Brian replied, with a grin. 'What has you down in this place? And where exactly are we?'

'Really?' laughed Eoin. 'Do you not recognise the place at all? It's Clonmel.'

Brian stopped and stared all around him. He picked out a landmark in the distance.

'There's the spire of St Mary's over there, I suppose. But no, there was no Gaelic club in this place when I grew up here. We used to play in a ground nearer the centre of town.'

'We're here to play a couple of games this morning. How did you get here?'

'Oh, the usual – I was having a ramble around Lansdowne Road when suddenly I was whisked away and found myself on the other side of that hedge. I spotted the goalposts and came to check it out. And then you appeared.'

Eoin had been the first person in almost ninety years to even see Brian when they met at the ground in Dublin on a school tour. They had last met on the field after an Ireland rugby international in Croke Park.

'I haven't seen you since that day in Croker,' Eoin replied. 'Have they fixed up Lansdowne Road yet?'

'It's a big job, I hear the workmen saying. But they're lashing into it anyway. So, how's your summer gone. Did I hear you went to New Zealand?'

Eoin started to tell Brian the story of his tour with the Lion Cubs, but he was disturbed by a loud whistle and a call from Paddy.

'Madden, what are you doing up that end? Come down here for the warm-up!' he shouted.

'Gotta go, I'll see you later,' Eoin told Brian before jogging off down towards the clubhouse.

Paddy didn't look very happy, but Eoin told him he

was just off doing a few stretches and sprints and he seemed to forgive him.

'Right, team, this is just a challenge match, so don't go wild, and remember we have another game afterwards,' said Paddy. 'It's been a while since we had a football team so I just want you to enjoy it. Let's try to keep the ball moving and be on the lookout for scores. Now, out you go.'

Eoin lined up in the middle of the field and waited for the referee to throw the ball in. Being taller than his team's other midfielder, Ultan, Eoin stepped forward to jump for the ball.

The referee tossed up the ball, and Eoin leapt into the air and clutched onto the leather. As he dropped to earth he felt a sharp pain in his side as his opponent elbowed him in the ribs. The ball slipped from his grasp as Eoin stumbled and fell, and the Clonmel centre-fielder collected it and raced away towards the goal.

Eoin stood up and rubbed his side and watched as the player who elbowed him played a pass through to the Clonmel full-forward who smashed the ball over for a point.

'Hey ref, did you not see our fella getting a dig at the throw-in?' roared Dylan, but the official just ignored him and took note of the score in his notebook.

Dylan put his arm across Eoin's back as his friend gathered himself.

'That was a sneaky blow, I'll get him back for you,' said Dylan.

'No, don't,' said Eoin replied. 'Shouting at the ref wasn't a great idea, now he's going to have his eye on you looking for an excuse to give you the sideline.'

Dylan snorted. 'I'd like to see that.'

CHAPTER 8

Ormondstown, like most of those in Tipperary, was mostly a hurling club. The boys hadn't played much football all year, and it showed. Clonmel quickly went into a four points to nil lead and too many of Eoin's team looked completely unused to even the basic skills of kicking a ball.

Eoin had at least that much, and he decided early on that there was little point passing the ball as Ormondstown's forwards were even worse than the backs.

He enjoyed the new challenge and found himself using some of the skills he had developed in rugby, like sidestepping, to get past the opposing defence.

On one of the few occasions he was able to get the ball, Eoin set off for goal, remembering to bounce the ball or solo it – tap it off his boot – every four steps so he was allowed to continue his run. Once he got within range he shook off the full back and flipped the ball onto the ground where he drop-kicked it high and straight between the posts for a point.

On the Gaels team there was a mixture of delight that they had finally broken their duck on the scoreboard, and amusement that Eoin had brought one of his rugby skills to bear on their game.

The Clonmel lads were united however – and they all roared laughing at the drop-kick.

'Ye're the rugby lad aren't ye?' one of them taunted Eoin.

'Yeah, I saw him on the telly,' said another.

'Well keep your scrums and drop-kicks to rugby,' sneered a third.

Eoin turned his back on them and walked into his position to await the kick-out.

'Watch it, Eoin,' came a call from Dylan, and Eoin turned his head in time to avoid a swinging punch from the midfielder who had elbowed him earlier.

'Hey, what's the story?' called Eoin, as his opponent gathered himself.

'Nothing. You just deserved that, you Dublin jackeen,' came the reply.

Dylan came racing up and stood in front of the Clonmel player who towered seven or eight inches above him.

'C'mon, hit me so, c'mon?' he roared.

His opponent looked down and laughed at Dylan, who responded with a punch in the stomach.

Everyone stopped and stared for a second, and then all hell broke loose. Several members of the Clonmel team raced towards Dylan, and his Ormondstown team-mates rushed to defend him.

The referee stepped in and barked at them to stop, and after a few seconds more of pushing and shoving the fracas ended.

The official called on the two mentors.

'This is not acceptable in a supposedly friendly juvenile game like this,' he began. 'If it happens again I'm abandoning the match. I want both teams to line up and shake hands with the other team and the next hint of a shemozzle and I'm off and you can ref your own hurling match.

'And these two can cool down on the sideline until half-time,' he said, picking out Dylan and the boy he had struck.

'And you,' he said, turning to Eoin. 'Stay out of trouble, I'm watching you.'

Eoin's mouth opened … but he decided it was better not to reply.

'That's so unfair,' he thought. 'But don't worry, I'll stay

clear of it.'

The Clonmel keeper took the kick-out, but it only found Vladis, the Ormondstown left half-forward, who ran fifteen metres before kicking the ball over the bar.

'This is a comeback,' roared Matthew Phelan, the Ormondstown captain, 'let's keep this up.'

But Matthew was being a bit too optimistic. The Clonmel side were able to slow things down and controlled the game for the rest of the half, although they only added a single point as Isaac made a couple of excellent saves.

Half time arrived and the team came together in a group on the halfway line where they were joined by Dylan and Paddy, and the rest of the subs.

'Five points to two isn't bad at all – better than I expected – and I suppose we should thank Isaac for that,' Paddy said.

'We'd be even closer if Dylan had kept his head,' he added. 'That fellow that hit Eoin was a hothead and the ref would surely have sent him off anyway if you hadn't turned it into the Battle of Waterloo. You forced the ref to send the two of ye off.'

Dylan looked sheepish and apologised to Paddy and the team.

'OK, I'm going to move Eoin to half-forward, let's

look to getting the ball in to him. He's big and well able to handle the rough stuff.

'And stay out of trouble the rest of ye!'

CHAPTER 9

Dylan was back in position for the start of the second half, but Eoin noticed that Cormac – the lad who had taken a swing at him – had been substituted by his own coach.

Clonmel were better organised from the start and soon extended their lead by two points before Eoin had even touched the ball.

'We've no chance here,' Dylan said to him at a break in play.

'Maybe, but we can stir it up a bit for them,' grinned Eoin. 'Next time you get the ball slip it through to me on my right-hand side.'

Ormondstown kept it tight for the next while and Vladis scored a second point. But the Clonmel side were well-drilled and kept up a regular supply of ball to their forwards who took their points.

There was just a couple of minutes left on the clock

and with the Gaels losing by ten points most of their players' heads had dropped. Dylan won the ball at half-back and set off on a run, checking his options as he hopped the ball.

Ahead of him, Eoin darted out to the left of the goal and half turned to watch Dylan's progress. His friend spotted him and dropping the ball onto his boot, he kicked it through to Eoin's right-hand side as he had asked.

Without hesitation, Eoin swung his right foot as the ball arrived, connecting perfectly with his bootlaces. The ball swung into the air and curved past the goalkeeper into the top right-hand corner of the net.

This late consolation goal greatly cheered his team-mates, who celebrated as if they had won the game. Clonmel were stung by the setback and raced down the other end to score the final point of the game but Gaels were just as happy at the final whistle.

'Thanks for the game, lads,' Eoin said, shaking hands with some of the opposition.

'Sorry about that stuff earlier, our Cormac can get a bit hot in the head over football,' said one Clonmel player.

Eoin grinned. 'No worries, I'll have to find him and shake his hand.'

The two teams gathered in the hall for crisps and cans of soft drinks, and Paddy and the local chairman made short speeches welcoming the new links between the clubs.

'I'm also the chairman of the Tipperary county juvenile board,' said the Clonmel official. 'And we're trying to get football going in parts where it has been neglected. Last night we had a meeting and so I'm happy to announce that we've decided to hold a special two-day tournament this year for all the clubs in the county – and the Ormondstown Gaels have agreed to host it.'

Eoin and his team cheered the mention of their club name, and a busy conversation was struck up as every boy in the room discussed this development. Some were buzzed about the idea of a big competition in their hometown, others about a trip involving a stay over in another town.

After a while they wandered out to the field again, and the team Paddy selected began their warm-up for the hurling match. Eoin and Dylan had been left out of the starting fifteen so they rambled up the far end.

'I met Brian up here earlier,' Eoin told his friend. 'It's the first time I've seen him since Croke Park.'

Dylan was one of the few people who knew about Eoin's ghostly pal.

'Why did he turn up down here?' asked Dylan.

'I don't know,' replied Eoin.

'I don't know either,' said Brian, suddenly appearing at Dylan's shoulder.

'Don't do that appearing thing without warning!' said Dylan, 'you nearly frightened the breakfast out of me.'

'Sorry, Dylan,' grinned Brian. 'But I'm not sure I can control that.'

'Were you watching the game?' asked Eoin. 'We were pretty brutal, but the two of us combined for a cracking goal at the end.'

'No, I was off wandering around the town. It's changed a lot since I was a boy, but it was great to see the Friary and the old walls once again. I even saw a road sign for a rugby club out the road.'

'No, seriously, WHY are you here?' asked Dylan.

Brian shrugged his shoulders.

'Usually when I appear to Eoin it is because there's something brewing. Some mystery or danger. Or something he needs my help on,' he replied.

'Is there anything going on?' he asked, turning to Eoin.

'Not that I know of,' answered Eoin, screwing up his face trying to think of what might have caused Brian to be called.

'It was hardly that Cormac fella, was it?' asked Dylan.

'Nah, I didn't need Brian for that — sure I had you,' laughed Eoin.

CHAPTER 10

The referee blew his whistle to get the hurling match started, and Brian, Eoin and Dylan stood watching from the corner furthest from the clubhouse.

'I haven't seen hurling for a long time,' said Brian. 'They never played it in Lansdowne Road. The hurleys look a different shape to the ones we used to play with – the bit at the bottom is wider and rounder.'

'Really?' asked Dylan. 'I still find it hard to hit the ball, I'd say it was even harder in those days.'

Brian nodded. 'I wasn't much good at it to be honest, I played Gaelic football more, and then when I went to school up in Kildare I got into the rugby. And well, that was that.'

Ormondstown were much better at hurling and soon eased to a six-point lead, which they held until half-time.

'We can give a few of you other lads a run if you like,'

said Paddy, pointing along the line of substitutes.

Eoin nodded. 'I wouldn't mind ten minutes at the end if you want to leave one of the lads get a few extra minutes under his belt,' he said.

Paddy grinned.

'Minutes? You're talking rugby language there, Madden,' he replied. 'But fair enough, I'll hold you back in case we let that lead slip.'

Dylan was happy enough not to be called on at half-time either, preferring to puck the ball around on the sideline with Eoin.

Brian waved them farewell and headed off through the ditch, leaving Eoin wondering when he might see him again.

Ormondstown continued to dominate the hurling match and were eight points clear when Eoin and Dylan were waved on with a few minutes left.

The Clonmel boys were battling hard, but in the last minute Isaac unleashed an enormous puck-out and Eoin rose to snatch it out of the air on the 45-metre line.

He turned quickly and raced in on goal, bouncing the sliotar on his hurl as two defenders rushed out to deal with him.

Eoin planted his left boot in the ground, and swivelled

around on his right leg, swerving past the defenders. He ran a few more steps before tapping the ball over the bar.

The ref's final whistle sounded immediately and Eoin was submerged by his team-mates.

'Brilliant, what a score!' said Matthew.

'You're a legend!' said Fintan.

Eoin looked completely bemused by the attention.

'Easy lads, sure we were winning by miles – one more point at the end is no big deal,' he said.

'Oh, but it is,' laughed Matthew. 'Did you not know what was going on?'

'Yeah,' said Isaac with a huge grin. 'We lost the football by eight points, but we won this one by nine. That means we win the cup!'

Eoin blushed – he hadn't been aware there was a cup up for grabs, let alone that it would be won by the team who scored the most over the two games.

The teams shook hands, and the officials came out carrying a large silver cup. One of the Clonmel seniors, who Eoin had seen play for Tipperary on television, presented medals to both sides.

'That's the first medal I've ever won for GAA,' laughed Eoin as they got changed in the clubhouse. 'I could get used to this.'

The bus journey back to Ormondstown flew by, with Dylan standing up on his seat near the front to lead the singing.

'We arrrrrrrre the champions, we are the champions... of all Tipp,' he roared, to the delight of his teammates.

'I wouldn't go as far as that,' said Paddy with a laugh as he ushered Dylan to sit back down.

'Now, listen up. That football tournament we're going to host is in three weeks' time,' said Paddy.

'We'll be training for it three days a week from now on, but we can't afford to slacken off the hurling either, so I don't want anyone taking holidays or anything like that.'

There was a groan from the back of the bus as a couple of the boys realised they would be away for the competition.

'And I also want all of you to give up a few hours of your time to help get the club looking ship shape – we can't have lads from Thurles or Roscrea looking down on us now for having a filthy club that needs a lick of paint, can we?'

Not long afterwards, the bus pulled into the car park at the Gaels. Eoin had texted Alan from the bus to tell him when they weren't far away and his pal was waiting at the door of the clubhouse when they arrived.

'Hey, Alan, good to see you,' called Dylan, still bubbling over with delight from the victory.

The trio exchanged hugs and fist bumps, and Dylan filled Alan in on the great win.

'How long are you staying for?' he asked his Castlerock schoolmate. 'It's just we have a big football tournament coming up and we're down a few men. You'd definitely get your place on the bench, at least.'

Alan's face turned pale.

'Football? Like soccer? – Or is it Gah?' he asked.

Eoin laughed at his friend's horror-stricken expression.

'Ah, Alan, it's not that bad. Gaelic is a bit like soccer or rugby, but they don't dive to tackle you around the legs, and there's no scrums or line-outs or any of that lark that you hate so much. AND the ball is round so you don't get awkward bounces. You'll pick up the rules quick.'

Alan seemed slightly reassured by that, and Dylan and Eoin lifted their gear bags onto their shoulders and turned towards the gate out of the car park for the long walk home.

'Hang on, where are you going?' asked Alan.

'Home? Where else?' asked Eoin.

'Yeah – well your mother is here in the car to collect you,' he answered, pointing over to where Eoin's mother was sitting waiting for them.

'She doesn't usually collect me when I'm down here,' replied Eoin, puzzled.

'Well... I suppose I might have asked her for a lift,' said Alan. 'I didn't think I would be able to walk that far after eating three slices of her apple tart.'

CHAPTER 11

Alan took the spare bed in Eoin's room, the bed that was buried beneath a stack of kit bags, rugby shirts and various items he had gathered on his travels.

'Cool, that's a real All Blacks shirt, isn't it?' asked Alan, picking it off the bed.

'Yeah, well, it's the Baby Blacks, I suppose,' Eoin replied. 'I swapped with their out-half after the second Test.'

Alan was impressed by the full set of jerseys from the other Six Nations sides that Eoin had also collected.

'Do you have one of the Clonmel team?' he asked, with a grin.

Eoin tossed a t-shirt in the direction of his pal.

'Now, now, none of that talk. We had a good game, and we won a trophy, which wasn't bad for a Saturday morning. What have you won this summer?'

Alan looked at his toes. 'Well, I did win a prize at a

rugby summer camp…'

'Really? Fair play Al, what was it for? Nicest woolly hat?'

'No, actually,' his friend retorted. 'It was a special rugby coaching camp, and I got the highest marks. They gave me a cool signed Ireland jersey as a prize.'

'Well done, buddy, that's fantastic. Was it your famous notebook that clinched it for you?'

Alan grinned. He was a pretty useless rugby player, but had made himself invaluable to the team at Castlerock College by studying how his squad and their opponents played. His analysis proved vital in their winning trophies and he had even helped Eoin and his team when he was playing for Ireland Under 15s.

'Yeah, they were impressed by how I looked at things a bit differently to the usual stuff. I'm going to do a coaching course when we get back to school.'

'Wow, and then maybe you'll take over from Mr Carey for the Senior Cup?'

Alan laughed. 'You've got to be joking. No chance. But it's something I'd like to get into when I'm older. I love the game, but I know I'm a terrible player.'

The pair cleared off the bed and moved Eoin's rugby shirt collection into a black plastic bag.

'Will we head down to the middle of town and meet

up with Dylan and Isaac?'

'Yeah, sounds good – who's Isaac,' asked Alan.

Eoin explained about their friend, who had moved from Africa to Ireland when he was small and moved again to Ormondstown the year before.

'He's a great lad,' said Eoin. 'He's a class goalkeeper and he's going to join me and Dylan in our gardening company.'

'Eh? What's your gardening company?' asked Alan.

'Oh yeah, me and Dyl made a few euro working in Grandad's garden. We reckon we could get a good summer job out of doing it round the town.'

Alan frowned. 'Hmmm, I thought we were going to have a bit of crack exploring and playing ball,' he said. 'That all sounds a bit like hard work.'

'Ah Al, I won't be working on that all day, just a few mornings here and there. You might enjoy it, it's great exercise.'

Alan wasn't convinced, but agreed that a trip into town would be a good idea.

They were strolling past the library on the way to Dylan's house when they noticed Isaac running towards them, looking back over his shoulder every few metres.

'Isaac, what's up?' asked Eoin.

'That Rocky and his gang, they hopped on me and Vladis outside Superburgers and took his money,' he replied, panting.

He leaned over and put his hands on his knees to get his breath back.

'I ran as fast as I could... they were chasing me... but they must have given up,' he told them.

'Is there a police station around here? You should tell the Garda,' suggested Alan.

Isaac smiled thinly. 'Fat lot of good that would do. Rocky's father is a guard so nothing's going to happen to him.'

CHAPTER 12

Eoin, Alan and Isaac called down to Dylan's house where his sister Caoimhe opened the door again.

'Hiya Ki, is the star footballer here?' asked Eoin, with a grin.

Caoimhe smiled and invited them in.

'He's upstairs, having a nap. He says it's what all the footballers do with their afternoons.'

'I hope he's not planning to stay in bed when we get the gardening started?' said Eoin.

'I heard that,' called Dylan, as he came down the stairs. 'I was just taking a rest – I played two matches today in case you didn't notice?'

'Two? You squeaked on for five minutes at the end of the hurling!' laughed Eoin.

'Anyway, what are you up to Dyl?' asked Alan. 'Eoin's going to show me the sights of Ormondstown – though so far it seems a bit rough.'

Isaac texted Vladis to check he had got away safely, and then explained to Dylan what had happened to him.

Dylan's temperature started to rise. 'We have to sort that crowd out,' he snapped.

'Look, there's not much point, the gang leader's dad's a guard, and we'll be back at Castlerock before too much longer,' said Alan.

'Yeah, but what about Isaac, and the rest of the lads on the team?' said Dylan. 'They have to live in the same town as them all the year round.'

'Good point, Dyl,' said Eoin. 'We'll have to see what we can do. It won't be easy though.'

The four boys headed down to the town centre, and they introduced Alan to their local burger restaurant.

'We don't have any Superburgers shops in Dublin,' he said, warily, as they walked through the door.

'Ah, you'll be fine, they kill the cattle out the back so you can be sure the meat is very fresh,' said Dylan.

Alan's face turned pale again, and he ordered a veggie burger instead.

'Good idea, Al,' said Eoin, who had been cutting down on meat himself. 'I'm thinking of become totally vegetarian when I get back to school. Mam won't hear anything of it while I'm here though.'

'Yeah, if you saw how the animals had to live before they end up on your plate you'd never eat meat again,' said Isaac, who ordered the same as Alan.

'Well, I think there's nothing like a tasty burger,' said Dylan, taking care to fish out the tomato and lettuce before he took his first bite.

The boys finished their meal, discussing whether they preferred football or hurling after their trip to Clonmel.

'It's easier to save the football,' said Isaac, 'but you don't have a hurl to protect yourself with.'

'I love the feeling of hitting a sliotar squarely and cleanly,' said Eoin, 'but I think I found it easier to get the hang of football better having played so much rugby.'

'Yeah, I get that,' said Dylan, 'but it's nice to have a big stick in your hand to slap the ball with. It's like hitting someone without getting into trouble.'

Alan grinned at them. 'Well, having never tried either of them, I must say they both look and sound a bit violent.'

'And you like rugby?' asked Isaac, with a grin. 'There's a lot fewer injuries in the GAA, you know.'

'Well I'll give the football a go, anyway,' replied Alan. 'The idea of being on the same field with Dylan carrying a lethal weapon doesn't appeal to me very much.'

CHAPTER 13

The boys knocked around town for a while, but Eoin could see Isaac was a bit nervous and kept looking up and down the street, obviously worried that his tormentors might return. Eoin felt sorry for his pal, but was also angry that someone had to live in such fear.

'Don't worry Isaac,' he told him. 'We have your back.'

He suggested they head home, and on the way they all made a detour to first leave Dylan home and then bring Isaac to his door safely. As Isaac's apartment was close to Dixie's cottage, Eoin suggested to Alan that they call in to see his grandfather before they went home.

'Good evening, Eoin – and Alan, isn't it?' said Dixie, as he showed them into his home. 'I'm sorry the place is in a bit of a mess, I nodded off in front of the television and never got my chores done.'

Eoin brought the dirty dishes into the kitchen, picked the newspapers off the couch, and sat down on it alongside Alan.

'No worries, Grandad, what else did you get up to today?'

Dixie sighed. 'Not much, I'm afraid. I did the shopping, had a lovely stroll around the garden admiring the work you and Dylan did, and then came in to read the papers and watch the racing... And then I fell asleep until you called.'

'That's a pity – you should have come down to Clonmel to watch us,' said Eoin. 'We won a trophy because we beat them at hurling by more than they beat us at football.'

'Yeah, you won on aggregate,' said Alan. 'They have that in soccer too.'

Dixie smiled. 'Very good. You're certainly playing a wide range of sport this summer, Eoin.'

They chatted for a few minutes more, but decided not to stay when Dixie offered to make tea.

'We'll be back tomorrow, Grandad, I think Mam wants to take us all out for lunch somewhere and maybe go for a drive.'

Back at home, Eoin's mum had a huge dinner waiting for them, so the boys never mentioned that they had been to Superburgers.

'I thought you'd be hungrier than that,' his mum said as she watched them struggle to eat their meals. 'I'll have to leave the apple tarts for tomorrow so.'

Alan took the hint, and just about found room to hoover up the last of the carrots and broccoli on his plate.

'Just a small slice, please, Mrs Madden,' he said, as he brought the plate out to the dishwasher.

'Well now, Alan, you know full well there's no such thing as a small slice of apple tart in this house. So, cream or ice cream?'

Next morning the boys were still full after their enormous meal the night before and decided to skip breakfast and run down to Dixie's instead of waiting for a lift.

Eoin knew that Alan wasn't a fast runner, so he jogged along gently while his friend tried to keep up.

'We need to go easy on the apple tart,' Eoin suggested. 'We'll be in no shape for the tournament if Mam keeps force-feeding us that.'

Alan nodded, a little reluctantly, and leaned against the gate as they arrived at Dixie's home.

'I suppose so, I'm a bit out of condition from sitting

at home all summer. If you promise not to go too fast I wouldn't mind going out for a run every day.'

'That's a deal,' said Eoin. 'There's loads of great places to run around here. We'll do them all.'

They knocked at the door a couple of times, but there was no answer. Eoin went around the back of the cottage to see if Dixie was in the kitchen, but all he found was the back door wide open.

He walked in, calling his grandfather's name and heard a reply of 'I'm here' coming from the bedroom.

He knocked on the door and entered, and found his grandad was still in bed.

'I'm sorry, Eoin, I've had a bit of a shock,' the old man said. 'Do you have your phone with you? I need to ring the guards.'

'Why?' asked Eoin, handing over the mobile.

'I've had burglars,' he replied.

CHAPTER 14

'The little pups cut my landline off,' Dixie explained to Eoin, as he tapped the number of the local Garda station into his grandson's phone and waited for the call to be answered.

Dixie explained to the Guards what had happened and they checked he was okay and was with family before they hung up and told him they would be with him shortly.

'They told me to tell you not to touch anything,' Dixie told Eoin. 'I'll just get dressed before they arrive. Maybe give your dad a quick ring too?'

Eoin went to the front door and let Alan in before going back inside to phone his father, who said he would be there as soon as he could.

'The gardaí told him not to touch anything, so we better keep our fingerprints off the furniture,' Eoin told his friend.

'But we were here last night,' said Alan, 'our finger-prints will be everywhere.'

'I don't think we need to worry too much about that. Here's the gardaí,' he said, looking out the window.

Eoin's dad's car pulled up right behind the squad car, and both his parents leapt out.

'Grandad is in his bedroom, getting dressed,' Eoin told the two guards as he showed everyone into the house.

Eoin's parents looked very upset, but waited in the hallway until the gardaí were finished talking to Dixie.

'I've told you all I know,' Eoin said, frowning. 'Grandad said he'd had burglars, but the house doesn't look any messier than it was when we were here last night.'

After about ten minutes the local sergeant came out and told them that they had finished interviewing Dixie but that he had endured a frightening experience and should not be left alone for the rest of the day.

'You boys were here last night, Mr Madden has told me,' the sergeant said. 'Did you notice anyone hanging around outside at the time? Or do you notice anything different about the place this morning?'

Eoin shook his head. 'No, it all seems just as it was.'

Alan spotted something on the floor, just underneath the couch they had been sitting on the night before.

'I don't think that was there,' he said, pointing. 'It

looks like a black mobile phone.'

The sergeant stooped to pick up the phone carefully, using plastic gloves to make sure he didn't smudge any fingerprints.

'Put that in an evidence bag please,' he said to his colleague.

The other garda opened a plastic bag and put the phone inside before he lifted it up to the light to examine it. His eyes widened briefly before he put the bag into his pocket.

'Can we go into him now, please?' Eoin's mum asked the sergeant, who nodded in reply before thanking them all and leaving.

Dixie looked a little shaken by what had happened, but joined his visitors in the kitchen where Eoin's mother had made them all a pot of tea.

The old man explained that he had been woken up by the sound of someone opening the back door.

'I must have left it open last night, I was very tired,' he told them.

'I called out, asking who was there, but they didn't answer.'

He sipped at the tea and continued his story.

'Well, I decided to stay in the room here, but I couldn't find the key to lock myself in. So, these two young buckos came in with their hoods up and scarves over their faces – I think I heard another fellow outside moving around – and they were demanding money from me, and my phone.

'Well, I showed them my phone – it's got a wire attached to it so they weren't interested in stealing it, but they pulled it out of the wall so I couldn't call for help,' he told them.

'And did they touch you at all?' asked Eoin's father.

'No, they never came near me,' Dixie replied. 'They didn't say much, but they definitely had local accents and were quite young – not much older than Eoin.

'I gave them about twenty euro I had in my pocket, but they didn't get anymore. They were very nervous and left very quickly,' Dixie added.

'And did you sleep at all?' asked Mrs Madden, who looked very concerned.

'No, not until it got bright,' replied Dixie. 'I don't sleep much anyway, but I was afraid to get up so I decided to stay in bed till I heard people passing by on the road outside. But I fell asleep about seven o'clock I'd say and didn't wake up until Eoin came to rescue me.'

He smiled at his grandson, and gave him a thumbs up.

'As long as you're OK, Grandad,' Eoin said, biting his lip as he struggled with his fear for the old man and anger that he could be terrorised in his own home.

'Do you want me to call the doctor to get you checked out?' asked Eoin's father.

'No, no, no,' insisted Dixie. 'I'm fine. I'll have to be more conscious of security I suppose, but they did me no physical harm.'

The Garda sergeant came to the door of Dixie's bedroom.

'We're going to head off now. We wouldn't recommend that you be alone in the house for a few days. And try not to leave it unoccupied either. You have my number if you have any concerns or you remember anything about the intruders,' he told Eoin's grandfather.

The old man nodded and thanked the policemen.

'I'll stay for a few nights if you like Grandad – Alan and I can put down mattresses on the floor,' suggested Eoin.

'Now hold on a second young man,' interrupted his mother. 'Your grandfather has had a terrible fright and we don't want you interrupting burglars if they come back for another go,' she added.

CHAPTER 15

Eoin's father stepped in and suggested that they go out for lunch, but Dixie said he didn't want to leave the house.

'Maybe you could go off and get some food and the lads can stay here to mind me,' he suggested.

Eoin's parents went off to rustle up some lunch and the boys helped Dixie get comfortable in the living room.

'Stick on the television there, Alan,' suggested Dixie. 'There'll be a match on shortly.'

While Alan wrestled with the remote control, Eoin sat down beside Dixie.

'Do you think you know the robbers?' asked Eoin.

'I'm not sure,' replied Dixie. 'I didn't want to accuse anyone in the wrong, but there was something familiar about their leader.'

'Is he from Ormondstown?' asked Eoin.

'I'd bet a hundred pounds on it,' replied Dixie. 'His accent was just the same as you would hear up the town.'

'Do you think they'll come back?' asked Eoin.

'I doubt it,' said Dixie. 'I told them I didn't have any money and when they found I didn't have a mobile phone they seemed to lose interest.'

'They actually came out of here down a phone,' laughed Alan as he explained to Dixie how he had found the mobile.

'I wonder can the guards trace the owner?' he wondered.

'They can – and very easily,' said Alan. 'I'd say there's a good chance they've already identified him.'

Eoin decided to change the subject and their minds soon switched to the Gaelic football match on the television.

'I can't say I ever played that game,' said Dixie, 'We never had a chance in Dublin and by the time I came to live down here I wasn't interested in kicking any shape of football. They're keener on the hurling around here anyway. I used to go watch a few games when your dad played.'

'Dad?' asked Eoin, with a grin. 'I thought he was useless at all sports?'

'Well, that's not very nice ... but he was I suppose,'

replied Dixie.

'I remember he used to get distracted very easily. He'd often wander off into the corner and pick buttercups and daisies. Or spend more time watching the aeroplanes flying overhead.'

'I suppose sporting talent skipped a generation in your family,' said Alan, who knew all about Dixie's past as a brilliant rugby player.

'I don't know about that,' said the old man. 'Eoin's done a lot more than I have even at this stage. He could be very special indeed if he works at it.'

'Ah come on now, Dixie,' said Eoin. 'It will be a long time before they name a dorm after me in Castlerock.'

The old man smiled. 'Yes, that was a very nice thing of them. I think my old pal Andy Finn was behind it. I must give him a ring to let him know how you got on in New Zealand.'

'I'm sure he knows, Grandad,' said Eoin with a chuckle. 'They have this thing called the internet that allows you to find things out quickly. You can even get it on a mobile phone…. If you had a mobile phone.'

A knock came to the door before Eoin's parents let themselves in.

'We got a fine takeaway from the hotel,' said his mum. 'None of your Superburgers or any of that stuff.'

Eoin's dad lifted five huge plates covered in tin foil out of a paper sack and began to unwrap them.

Underneath were five steaming servings of turkey, ham and vegetables.

'It's Christmas in August!' said Alan, with delight.

Chapter 16

Eoin's dad stayed with Dixie when everyone else left, and the boys decided to start their fitness programme with a light jog to work off some of the enormous lunch.

Alan found it hard going. 'I... think... I... need... to—'

'—Stop eating apple tart?' suggested Eoin.

'No... just... just... STOP...' he said, as he leant up against a wall and caught his breath.

'I've been very lazy this summer,' he admitted. 'But if we do this every day I'll be OK to play a bit of Gaelic, I think,' he announced.

Eoin laughed. 'You make it sound like a gentle game of chess,' he said. 'I think we'll need to work harder than this to make you into an Ormondstown Gael.'

'Maybe they'd have room for an analyst?' suggested Alan, who had filled that role for their school and for

Ireland when Eoin had played the year before.

'Not a bad idea, although the fact that you have never even watched a game until two hours ago might be a bit of a drawback.'

'I have so watched GAA matches,' complained Alan. 'And I'll remind you that I'm from the county that has won more All-Ireland finals in the last ten years than anyone else. And I always watch the finals.'

Eoin agreed to give Alan a quick masterclass in the game using videos on the internet. But first, he wanted to call down to see Dylan and tell him about the burglary.

Caoimhe opened the door and invited them in.

'Hi, this is Alan,' he said, 'didn't you meet in Dublin a few years back?'

'Yep,' nodded Caoimhe, blushing a little. 'That was the time we had that scene with my dad at the Aviva Stadium.'

Dylan and his sister had been kidnapped briefly by their father, but Alan and Eoin had saved the day.

'Oh yes, sorry, I forgot,' said Eoin. 'Alan's down for a few weeks' holidays. We're showing him the sights of Ormondstown.'

'Sure we showed him all there was to see last night,' said Dylan, as he slid down the bannister that ran alongside the stairs.

'Careful with that, Dylan,' his mother snapped. 'You won't be much use to Eoin and the football team if you have a nasty fall.'

Dylan shrugged and grabbed his coat.

'If I broke my arm I'd still be a better footballer than half the team,' he replied with a grin. 'Probably even a better one-handed hurler too.'

The trio wandered around Ormondstown which, being a Sunday afternoon, was very quiet. There was a low-key hurling match taking place in the Gaels so the boys wandered in and found a secluded spot away from the clubhouse to watch the game and have a chat.

Eoin filled Dylan in on Dixie's terrible night.

'That's funny that they asked him for his phone, sure old lads like him don't have fancy mobiles at all,' offered Dylan.

'Yeah, Dixie's never really mastered them,' said Eoin.

'They lost one of their own phones too,' said Alan. 'A horrible black one with a skull on the back.'

Dylan's eyes widened, but just nodded and didn't say anything.

'Dixie thinks they're young fellas from around the

town,' said Eoin.

'That's not a bad guess,' replied Dylan, 'but they'll be hard to catch.'

As they were chatting, Paddy strolled out from the clubhouse to meet them. He was carrying three black plastic sacks and three pairs of gloves.

'Aren't you three very quick off the mark,' he announced, with a grin. 'When I was looking for volunteers to clean up the place I didn't think you would be down the very next day – and on a Sunday too. Well, fair play to you, boys.'

He held his arm outstretched to Dylan, handing him a bag and a pair of gloves, which the youngster took with a scowl.

'And for you Eoin,' he said, handing over another set, 'and one for your pal here. I couldn't see who it was from over at the clubhouse, but I'm sure you won't mind helping out, member or not?' he said to Alan, his grin widening.

'No problem,' said the visitor, 'I'm Alan. I'm at school with the lads up in Dublin.'

'Ah, so you'll be playing on our football team so, all those Dubs think they're world beaters at the Gaelic football.'

'Eh, this one doesn't,' admitted Alan. 'In fact, I've never

played a game of it. Ever.'

'Oh well,' Paddy sighed, disappointed. 'For a second there you had me thinking we might have unearthed a new star.

'Still, you look like you know what litter looks like. When the three of you fill those bags will you drop them back behind the clubhouse?' he asked, before pointing out the crisp bags that had got caught in the bushes and the discarded drink cans.

'I'll see you tomorrow for training,' he added, before heading back to watch the match.

CHAPTER 17

Next morning the boys headed back to the Gaels, where Paddy was waiting for them with a paper bag in his hand.

'Lads, I was delighted to see you had done so much collecting last evening. Here's a tin of fizzy stuff and a bag of crisps for each of you. Just make sure to stick them in the recycling bins when you're finished,' he grinned.

The boys thanked Paddy and joined the rest of the team in the dressing room.

Dylan looked around. 'Where's Isaac?' he asked.

'He texted me to say he was waiting for a lift and he'll be here as soon as he can,' said Finn.

'A lift?' said Dylan. 'Sure, he lives about five minutes away! We're nearer than him.'

Finn shrugged. 'He's a bit freaked out about Rocky and his gang,' he said. 'I think they really got to him over the weekend.'

'Sure, why didn't he get us to collect him? He can't let them ruin his summer,' Dylan replied.

Isaac walked into the dressing room and everyone went silent.

'Were you just talking about me?' he asked.

'Well… I was just saying that you can't be running around trying to avoid Rocky all the year round – we're going to have to sort that out,' said Dylan.

Isaac looked at the floor.

'That's easy for you to say Dyl, you're off to your posh boarding school in Dublin at the end of the month and don't have to live here.'

The boys had a good training session and Paddy had some help from Gareth, one of the senior team who had played a lot of football.

'There's a fair bit of talent there, Paddy,' he said as they all gathered outside the clubhouse at the end of the morning. 'I think we could do half decent in that blitz we're having. That rugby lad is very useful on the half forward line and with a good keeper you've the makings of a competitive team.'

Paddy nodded and thanked Gareth for his help.

'You heard the man there now, so let's all work harder

on getting it right. Same time tomorrow and no stragglers – be on time!' he added.

Walking back towards town, the boys discussed the training and Alan got an amount of teasing over how badly he had played.

'I think I'd fancy that job as the lad who carries on the water bottles,' he decided, announcing his immediate retirement from actually playing Gaelic football.

Isaac, Dylan and Eoin laughed at their pal, who had just had the shortest career of anyone in any sport.

As they reached the edge of town Dylan and Isaac took the turn off towards their homes and Alan and Eoin walked on.

Outside the bank they noticed the garda who had been in Dixie's house the day before. The officer was writing out parking tickets and putting them under the windscreen wipers of several cars.

'Excuse me, Guard,' said Alan. 'We met yesterday at the burglary at Dixie Madden's cottage. 'I was the one that found the mobile phone under the couch.'

The garda looked at Alan suspiciously.

'Yes….' he started.

'Well, I wonder have you been able to put a trace on it

– it's very easy to find who owns those things nowadays,' replied the youngster.

The garda finished writing the last parking ticket, tore it from the book and slipped it into place on the windscreen of an SUV.

'Mobile phone….' he muttered slowly.

'Yes,' said Alan, 'it was black, with a skull.'

The garda's face darkened. 'I don't recall anything of the sort being found. There was a small mobile telephone found, but there was no skull or crossbones on it. You must have been mistaken,' he snapped.

Alan took a step backwards.

'OK,' he said. 'I was only trying to help. I presume you found the owner of that phone though?'

'That's Garda business,' he said, curtly. 'But we have no reason to believe the owner was the burglar. It had been reported missing by a little old lady from up the town.'

'But… but…' started Alan.

'But nothing,' said the garda. 'Now, please leave us to do our jobs and stop interfering in a Garda investigation. That's a serious crime in itself,' he added, with a snarl.

CHAPTER 18

The boys spent the afternoon lounging around Eoin's kitchen trying to come up with names for the new gardening company.

After trying Green Machines, Cutting Hedge and the Lawn Rangers, Isaac finally came up with Blooming Magic.

Alan offered to draw up a logo and started playing around on Eoin's laptop designing a flyer to hand around the local houses and shops.

BLOOMING MAGIC

Local students available
for summer gardening work
Lawns, hedges, digging and weeding

Contact 020-911 5827
Dylan, Isaac, Eoin and Alan

'That's class,' said Dylan. 'I suppose my name should be on a separate line – and in bigger print – seeing as I'm the owner of the company?'

'Steady now,' said Eoin. 'If that's the case I'll be expecting to be get paid for every day of the week – not just the ones we have a job on. I'm sure Isaac would be the same too.'

Dylan went white. 'Ah… he said, we better not make it a company so – more like a co-op. Would that be OK by you?'

The rest of the boys grinned.

'Grand, so we're all in it together – equal shares?' said Isaac.

Dylan nodded. 'Yeah, I suppose you're right. But I don't want to see anyone shirking or staying late in bed in the mornings if we have a job to do.'

Eoin roared laughing. 'Staying late in bed? Says the man who has to be dug out of the mattress by a JCB most mornings?'

Dylan grinned, a bit sheepishly. 'Yeah right, so. You got me there.'

Alan laid the advert out so there were two flyers on each page and printed out a hundred sheets of paper. Eoin cut them in half while Dylan and Isaac studied a map of the town, working out which houses had the biggest gardens and would be most likely to give them the work.

'I have a route planned out here,' said Dylan. 'The big gardens are all down by the church there, and out the Dublin Road. There's a few of the new estates that might be worth hitting too, but we'll leave them for the second round if these don't work.'

Eoin snipped the final sheet in two and placed a neat stack of two-hundred handbills on the table.

'Right, so let's do this in teams of two, just in case there's any troublemakers around the town,' suggested Dylan. 'Isaac and I will go up to the Dublin Road as that's near where we live, and you pair head up around the posh houses on Church Road.'

The boys agreed to the plan and split up to do their deliveries.

'That's a brilliant idea,' said one man who was washing his car in his drive when Eoin and Alan showed him the flyer.

'Would you be able to cut the grass around the back and trim back those hedges? If you can do it tomorrow I'll pay you double as we have some people coming from England to stay for a few days.'

Eoin made an appointment for half past nine the next morning and assured the man his work would be done.

The boys got plenty of positive reactions to their new venture and even secured a couple of bookings for later in the week.

'We'll hardly have time to play football with all this work,' said Alan as they finally trudged up the path to Eoin's home.

Eoin stopped dead. 'Oh no, we have training in the morning and I've agreed to cut that man's lawn and hedges.'

'We could turn up early,' suggested Alan, 'and then you three all scarper off for an hour and I'll hold the fort. We should be able to get all the work done in time.'

When they arrived in the kitchen they discovered Eoin's dad had gone down to stay with Dixie so they sat and chatted with his mum until it was bedtime.

As they were getting ready for bed, Eoin's phone buzzed with a text. 'How did u get on' read the message from Dylan.

'Gr8,' Eoin replied. 'Got 3 jobs booked and 1 man said he'd pay double if we do it tmrw. U?'

'Got two on Weds. We hav GAA training tmrw tho.'

'I kno,' wrote Eoin, 'We'll hav to just juggle it and Al says he can stay dere all day. Will u text Isaac and tell him we'll pick him up at 9 and we can get tools then.'

'Will do. Gud Night,' replied Dylan.

Eoin snapped the phone shut and laughed.

'Nine o'clock in the morning! I doubt if Dyl has seen that time since the holidays began.'

CHAPTER 19

True enough, Eoin had to knock hard on the door to get Dylan up as his mum and sister had gone off somewhere.

'Come on, Dyl!' he shouted through the letterbox as his friend walked slowly down the stairs.

'I don't think these early mornings are a great idea. Let's just take jobs from two to four in the afternoon,' Dylan suggested.

The boys set off for Isaac's at a jog and met their friend outside the apartment block where he lived.

'The shed is just around the back here,' he told them, leading the way to a creaky wooden structure that leaned against the back wall of the grounds.

Isaac pushed open the door and let out a cry.

'They're gone!' he wailed. 'The mower and all the other stuff. Someone's been in since yesterday and stolen it all!'

'How… who…' said Eoin, shaking his head.

'I bet that Rocky has something to do with it,' said Isaac.

'Let's not worry about that just now,' said Alan, 'We have a double paying customer who we have to be at in about twenty-five minutes. Anyone got any ideas?'

The boys realised they had a problem, but Dylan had a solution.

'What about Dixie?' he asked Eoin. 'Would he lend us his mower? He has a set of shears and a spade too.'

Eoin nodded. 'That's a great idea, Dyl, I'll ring my dad as he's around there now. I'll ask him to meet us up near the church.'

Isaac's face fell. 'Does that mean you won't need me in the gardening company then?'

Dylan looked at him and grinned. 'What? Just because you're not bringing anything useful to it anymore? Nah, Isaac, you're a strong lad – you can do the heavy lifting.'

Eoin's dad – and Dixie – agreed to help the Blooming Magic team and at half past nine on the dot the four began work on Mr McGrath's garden.

The boys worked well together and after an hour they had made good progress.

'We better head off soon,' Eoin said. 'Paddy really doesn't like it if we are late.'

At that moment the back door of the house opened, and out strode Mrs McGrath with an enormous tray.

'Good morning boys,' she announced. 'I hope you all enjoy a cup of tea – and I've baked some nice chocolate muffins too. You need fuel for all that hard work you're doing.'

Alan grinned and whispered to the rest, 'You guys head off now. I can cope with four muffins.'

Mrs McGrath poured out four cups of tea and offered them milk and sugar. When she had finished she sat down beside them.

'So, tell me about this little enterprise you've started. I understand we are your very first customers.'

Dylan explained how they had come up with the idea, and Mrs McGrath offered to pass on the flyers to her friends with a recommendation.

'That would be lovely, thank you,' replied Eoin. 'It will be nice to be busy over the long holidays.'

Dylan looked at him sideways with a weird grin and pointed at his wrist with the universal signal that time was now an issue.

At Eoin's lead the boys rushed through their tea and muffins.

'I'm afraid you'll have to excuse us Mrs McGrath, I just got a text there saying that we need to collect an extra lawnmower to speed things up. It's over in Roscrea so we will be gone for an hour or two. Alan will be staying to keep the job going.'

Mrs McGrath frowned. 'There doesn't seem to be much to be gained by an extra mower if three you are missing for the rest of the morning. You do know we need to have this finished today. It's very important.'

'Of course,' replied Eoin. 'But we'll be back as soon as we can.'

Alan picked up the tray and brought the cups back to the house, creating a diversion so Isaac, Dylan and Eoin could grab their kitbags and leave.

The trio set off at a jog to the Gaels.

'That was so bad to lie to that woman,' Eoin said, disgusted with himself.

'Ah she'll be fine,' said Dylan. 'The last I heard was Alan telling her how delicious her muffins were. He'll be in there eating cake with her all morning.'

'He better not,' said Eoin. 'We need him to keep the job moving till we get back.'

CHAPTER 20

The three boys arrived at Ormondstown Gaels about fifteen seconds before training was due to begin, earning a frown from Paddy, but nothing worse than that.

'You lads look like you've had a hard session already this morning,' said Gareth. 'No need for much of a warm-up so, just get your stretches done.'

Gareth was right – the hard work, and stress, of the morning had taken its toll on the trio and they didn't have their usual verve and energy as the session wore on.

After an hour Eoin and Dylan were dead on their feet, and although Isaac didn't have as much running to do as he spent most of his time in goal, he too was starting to make errors.

'Right you three, let's hear your excuses,' Paddy demanded as he singled them out at the end of the session. 'What were you up to before training?'

Dylan started to speak, but Eoin recognised the signs that his friend was about to make up some cock and bull story and interrupted him.

'We've started this gardening business,' Eoin explained. 'And there was a bit of a problem with the timing so we had to do that for an hour before we got here, and then we got delayed so we had to run to get here on time.'

'We're sorry, Paddy,' said Isaac, 'It won't happen again.'

Paddy frowned for a few seconds before breaking into a grin.

'Ah lads, I have to admire your enterprise – and thanks for your honesty Eoin – but you can't be turning up for training as exhausted as that.'

'I know,' said Dylan. 'We're going to make sure we only do it in the afternoons from now on.'

'Right so, but don't drive yourselves too hard. Rest is very important – so get yourselves to bed early, especially coming up to the tournament.'

The three promised Paddy they would and set off at a gentle pace once again for Mrs McGrath's garden. As soon as they got around the corner out of Paddy's sight they broke into a sprint.

Alan was cutting the hedges when they rejoined him but it was obvious that he spent most of the time since they left enjoying Mrs McGrath's home baking.

'Did you do any work at all?' snapped Dylan.

Alan grinned back at him. 'I did a bit,' he replied. 'More than you lot did anyway.'

'Look, let's get down to work,' Eoin said. 'We can finish this today if we put our backs into it.'

It was a hot day, and the hard work on top of a training session was no joke. Alan and Dylan needed to stop for a break every few minutes, but Eoin and Isaac kept working as hard as they could.

About one o'clock Mrs McGrath came out with another tray, this time with sandwiches and tall glasses of orange juice.

She looked around the garden, a little puzzled. 'Where's the second lawnmower?' she asked.

Eoin coughed. 'I'm very sorry, Mrs McGrath. There is no second lawnmower. We had an important training session and I just came up with that stupid lie to get away. I apologise.'

Mrs McGrath smiled.

'Thank you for that, Eoin, I'm glad you admitted it. And I don't mind at all. Training sessions are very important and I'm a big supporter of Ormondstown Gaels.

'By the way, my brother just called in to see me – he's just finishing his sandwich and will be out in a second. I think you might know him.'

The boys turned towards the back door just in time to see Mrs McGrath's brother walking out.

'Paddy!' said Dylan. 'Are you here with Mrs McGrath's brother?'

'I *am* Mrs McGrath's brother!' replied the trainer with a wide grin on his face. 'She mentioned on the phone that she had these young gardeners in and I had a fair idea who they might be. So, I came down to check you out.'

'They're doing great work to be fair,' said his sister. 'I'm very pleased. Another couple of hours and it will be done.'

'Great stuff,' said Paddy. 'And don't forget – get to bed early tonight.'

CHAPTER 21

The boys finished their cutting, mowing, trimming and clipping just in time. They heard the sound of Mr McGrath's car door slamming just as they put the last touches to the flower bed at the back wall.

'That's magnificent work,' announced the home owner as he wandered around examining what the Blooming Magic boys had done.

'They've been brilliant all day,' said Mrs McGrath, who had come out to join them.

'And so has Mrs McGrath,' said Alan. 'She kept us well fuelled all day with tea and her delicious cakes.'

'I'm delighted to hear that,' said her husband, 'though I hope she mentioned that I was the one who made the chocolate muffins while she was still in bed this morning?'

Mrs McGrath blushed and laughed it off.

'Whoever made them, they were top class,' grinned

Alan. 'I hope you need that grass cut again before we head back to school.'

Mr McGrath handed over two fifty euro notes to Eoin.

'This is the double fee for the work, as agreed, and I've added a five-euro bonus for each of you. And the best of luck with the rest of your summer.'

The boys were very grateful and thanked him before they packed up the rest of their equipment. Eoin texted his dad who came to collect the mower.

'Do you want a lift home, lads?' he asked.

The boys declined, preferring to walk home in the warm sunshine and chat about their successful foray into the world of commerce.

Isaac and Dylan were walking about ten metres in front of Eoin and Alan when they turned a right-hand corner into the main street of Ormondstown. By the time the second pair had reached the corner Isaac and Dylan were pressed up against a wall surrounded by four larger youths – Rocky and his gang.

'Hey, leave them alone!' Eoin shouted.

Rocky turned to face him. 'And this is the big rugby star, is it?' he sneered. 'You keep out of it, I'm just having a word with Isaac here and making sure he pays his tax.'

Eoin had seen enough of bullies in his school to know

there was no point backing down. He drew himself up to his full height and stepped forward.

'And I'm saying let them go. Isaac doesn't need to pay tax to anyone.'

'We have a special tax in this town for anyone who's not Irish – so keep out of it, pal.'

'Isaac is Irish, and anyway, whatever he or anyone else is doesn't give you the right to order him around. Now let him go.'

Rocky half turned to go back to his gang before switching back and unfurling a huge swinging punch.

Eoin ducked, and Rocky fell off balance. As he staggered to regain his feet, Eoin grabbed him by the shirt and lifted him off the ground and held him up against the wall.

'Did you ever hear the expression, "When you come at the King you best not miss"? … I thought not,' Eoin grinned.

'It's never a good idea to swing a punch if you're not sure you're going to take the man out.'

He went on: 'Now listen, I could smash you back against the wall here and put you in hospital for a week. But I'm not going to, because you're not worth it.

'You're a pathetic little bully, and the rest of your so-called gang know it too. When I eventually let you back down you're going to apologise to Isaac and that will be the last time you ever say a word to him. OK?'

Rocky nodded, and his friends stepped back from Isaac and Dylan.

Eoin dropped the bully to the ground, and he turned to Isaac.

'I'm sorry,' he muttered, before turning to walk away.

'You dropped this,' said Alan, handing Rocky back his mobile – a black shiny phone with a skull on the back – before the bully rejoined his gang as they wandered off.

CHAPTER 22

'Did you see his phone?' said Eoin. 'That was the one you found in Dixie's house wasn't it?'

Alan nodded. 'I'm sure of it, and that garda I gave it to must be Rocky's father.'

'So Rocky broke into your grandad's home?' said Isaac, with a gasp.

Eoin paused, feeling the anger rise inside him, but forcing himself to stay cool so he could work out what was best to do next.

'That's serious stuff,' said Dylan. 'I thought it might be when you mentioned the skull phone earlier, but didn't want to say unless I was sure. We need to say something to the guards.'

'But the garda must have given the phone back to him,' said Eoin. 'That's even more serious. And we don't really have any evidence.'

'Well... I might be able to dig some up. When Rocky

dropped his phone there I was able to pick it up without anyone seeing. When you were giving him that speech I quickly downloaded a tracker app and hid it in his phone. I have the code for the app so we will be able to keep tracks on wherever Rocky is at any time,' said Alan.

'That's brilliant, Alan,' said Eoin.

'Can I get the code too?' asked Isaac, 'it would be good to know where he was if I have to go up town on my own – just in case he's not a good listener, Eoin.

'Cracking idea, Al,' agreed Dylan. 'And we could find out if he and his gang have a hideout where they hide the stuff they steal too.'

The boys wandered around the shops for a while, but decided to save their first day's pay packet.

'Thanks again, Eoin,' said Isaac. 'We all worked so hard for that cash – it would have been heartbreaking to lose it all to that gang.'

'No worries, Isaac,' he replied. 'But remember – just stand up to him. You're nearly as big as he is now, and I bet you're a lot stronger. Stand up to him once and he'll back off forever.'

Alan twiddled with his phone and opened a new screen showing where Rocky's mobile – and Rocky – was now.

'They're down at the back of the nursing home,' said

Isaac. 'There's a little shed there right enough. Like an old storehouse. I bet that's where they have their den.'

'Well there's no point going there now,' said Eoin. 'Let's leave it till later in the week when we know they're not around.'

'I agree,' said Dylan. 'And I don't know about you guys, but I'm about to fall asleep and it's not even six o'clock yet. I'll definitely be taking Paddy's advice and getting to bed early tonight.'

Next day they had hurling practice, so Alan stayed in bed while Eoin hauled himself up and got ready for the session.

'Every part of me hurts,' he complained. 'I used muscles yesterday I've never used before and they're not happy with me.'

Isaac and Dylan had the same problem, but they decided they couldn't give up on Blooming Magic after one day.

'We can do the doctor's garden on Dublin Road today,' Dylan suggested. 'And the one across from there tomorrow.'

'How about we split up, though,' suggested Isaac. 'One pair does the lawn in one house while the other does the other work in the doctor's, then switch when we're finished. They're only a few metres away so it would be easy.'

'Great idea,' said Eoin, 'though it would be a lot easier if we had two mowers.'

The boys followed Isaac's suggestion and managed to get both jobs done. Although there weren't enough tools to go around Alan spent his spare time going around filling black plastic sacks with grass and hedge clippings. He then carried them on his shoulders, two at a time, down to the council recycling centre, which was about a five-minute walk away.

It meant they were all ready to go when the job was complete and they just had to return the tools to Dixie.

'We should be paying you for the hire of these,' Alan said as the old man welcomed them in.

'Not at all, Alan, I'm glad they're proving of some use to you,' his grandfather told them. 'Though I wouldn't mind the odd bit of free gardening done out the back...'

CHAPTER 23

After dinner Eoin texted Dylan and they all arranged to meet outside Isaac's apartment block.

'It's only starting to get dark,' Alan said when they got there, 'we should wait until the sun has completely gone down.'

The boys kicked a football around for a while until Alan decided it was time to leave.

'I've been checking the app regularly,' he told them, 'and Rocky has been at home since just after six o'clock. Looks like he might have been grounded.'

Eoin grinned. 'It has not been a good week for Rocky,' he said.

'And it could be about to get a lot worse,' chuckled Dylan.

The boys followed Isaac as he led the way down to the shed that Alan had identified as the hideout.

It was a dark corner of the complex and the boys

moved carefully and silently, afraid they might wake up some of the elderly residents of the home.

When they reached the shed door, Alan switched on the flashlight app on his mobile and tried the handle of the door.

'It's locked,' he said.

The boys searched for another entrance but had no luck.

'Hang on,' said Dylan, pointing down at the path that led up to the shed. He had spotted a stone slab with a small skull painted on it and slipped his fingers around the edges to lift it up.

There underneath the slab was a small brass key.

'Bingo!' said Isaac. 'Great spot, Dyl.'

Eoin picked up the key and slipped it into the lock, twisting it and hearing a satisfying click.

The boys entered quickly and soon filled almost the whole of the floor space inside.

The rest was taken up with bikes, boxes of computer games and mobile phones – and several pieces of gardening equipment.

'That's the stuff from Mr Kearney's shed,' gasped Isaac. 'They must have nicked it!'

Eoin picked up a small silver clock.

'This is from Dixie's – I don't think anyone even

noticed it was gone. Look, his name is carved on the bottom. He got it from his rugby club many years ago.'

'We should ring the cops,' said Dylan. 'There's lots of other stuff here.'

'We should do it without giving our name – and not to Rocky's father either,' said Isaac.

The boys agreed a strategy – they took the mower and shears and put them in Dixie's shed until they could get a lock for the door of old Mr Kearney's.

When they finished there, they stopped in the park near the old castle. Alan had taken one of the phones that was still charged from the box in the gang hut and switched it on. The code '0000' didn't work but '1234' did. Almost everyone uses those numbers, he had read somewhere.

'OK everyone, keep quiet for a minute,' he said, as he dialled the number for the local Garda barracks. 'I hope I don't get Rocky's dad.'

The phone rang for half a minute before it was answered.

'This is Ormondstown Garda Station, how can I help you?' came a voice.

'Eh, is that the sergeant?' Alan asked, putting on a strange mixture of a Cork accent mixed with one from California.

'It is the sergeant,' came the reply, 'and who is this?'

'Oh, I'm just a tourist passing through your town, but I think I have a crime to report,' Alan went on. 'I've just been in the nursing home on a visit and went out for a walk. I came across an old shed with a key in the door so of course my curiosity got the better of me and I let myself inside.'

Eoin and Dylan had to pinch themselves to stop laughing at Alan and his stupid story – and even more stupid accent.

'Now this no ordinary workman's shed – it was full of bikes and boxes of cell phones, x-box games and a silver clock with the name of Dixie Madden engraved on it. He's the old guy whose house was burgled I heard,' Alan added.

'Where did you hear that?' asked the sergeant.

'Oh, about the town,' said the mystery caller. 'Even I've heard of Dixie Madden and I'm from Sligo,' he added.

'Sligo?' replied the garda. 'That doesn't sound very Sligo to me – I could have sworn you were a Yank. What's your name, so?'

Alan panicked. 'Eh, no I'm not a Yank. I'm from Sligo – Ben is my name. Ben Bulben.'

'Well thank you very much Mr Bulben,' replied the

sergeant, sarcastically. 'I'll take a spin down there and check that out. You've been very helpful. Do you have a phone number I can contact you at, or an address?'

Alan hit the button to end the call.

'Too many questions, sergeant,' he said, still in the funny voice. 'I'm not the one you need to be asking the questions.'

CHAPTER 24

The next day Isaac and Dylan organised a padlock and secured Mr Kearney's garden shed. Having a second mower and set of shears was a great boon to Blooming Magic and they were able to do a lot more work – and plenty had started flooding in since Mrs McGrath had put the word around about how good they were.

When they weren't gardening they were training, and even Alan had started coming along. Eoin's pal spent his evenings studying videos of All-Ireland finals on You-Tube and working out the tactics and what to look for in a good player.

'Come and look at this lad Bernard Brogan,' Alan suggested to Eoin. 'He was Dublin's full forward for years – look at the way he moves into positions and gets ready to collect the ball. If you and Dylan could get something like that going?'

Eoin watched the videos as the footballer picked off points and smashed in goals from all angles. He enjoyed one he scored when his team-mate fired a shot across the goal which was going wide and Brogan stuck his foot out and steered the ball into the net. He promised Alan he'd study the videos more, but right now he needed a lot of sleep.

As they counted down the days to the tournament the Blooming Magic work started to dry up, so they were delighted when Paddy took the four boys aside after the final training session on Thursday morning.

'We've no training tomorrow lads, we've done all the work we can to turn you into a decent football team. But I wonder would you be up for turning this place into a decent football venue?'

'What do you mean?' asked Dylan.

'The committee were talking about you last night – you've done half their gardens – and wonder would you be free to do a bit of a tidy-up around here – not cutting the pitch but all the other areas that need a trim as well as getting the ditches cleaned up too. We'll pay ye!'

'Well… OK,' said Dylan. 'I suppose we could do that.'

'We'll only charge mates' rates,' said Eoin. 'We couldn't take the full fee off you.'

'Eh, hang on….' Dylan started, but thought better

of it. 'Grand so, we'll bring the gear down first thing tomorrow.'

The boys were glad of the extra work, but not of the exhaustion they felt at the end of the day making the Ormondstown Gaels grounds spick and span for the weekend.

'How are we supposed to play football tomorrow?' Eoin asked Alan as he stashed the mower back in Dixie's shed.

Alan grinned. 'That's not my problem – although I suggest you get plenty of sleep. That seems to be Paddy's solution to everything.'

Eoin knocked on the door of his grandfather's cottage and was delighted to find him in.

'Come in, come in,' said Dixie. 'I've some exciting news for you.'

Alan joined Eoin on the couch as Dixie went to put the kettle on.

'I had a visitor here not so long ago,' the old man told them as he came back into the room. 'The Garda sergeant.'

The boys' eyes widened. 'What did he want?' asked Eoin.

'Nothing – he actually brought something back to me,' replied Dixie, reaching over to the mantelpiece and lifting down his silver clock.

'I never noticed it was gone, but the burglars must have taken it that night. The sergeant said they had recovered it as part of an investigation but couldn't tell me where or who is involved. I'm glad to have it back I suppose but it's still all a bit of a mystery. I hope they catch them all the same.'

Eoin looked at Alan, but they decided not to tell Dixie what they knew.

'That's fantastic, Dixie,' said Alan. 'But how did they know it was your clock?'

'Good question,' Dixie replied. 'My old rugby club gave it to me when I was picked by Leinster – my name is engraved on it somewhere.'

With the subject successfully changed, Alan continued to ask Dixie about his time playing for the province and they soon whiled away an hour listening to the old man's sporting memories.

'I'll be down to see you make a few sporting memories of your own over the weekend, of course,' said Dixie. 'What time is this blitz on at?'

Alan explained that the games would go on from about noon till 6pm on Saturday, and 10am to 3pm on

Sunday. 'I think they're planning to let everyone watch the All-Ireland hurling semi-final then and have the final afterwards but we can't guarantee Ormondstown will be there,' he added.

'I suppose I'd better call down early tomorrow so,' chuckled Dixie. 'Just in case you're knocked out early.'

CHAPTER 25

The Ormondstown boys met up at ten o'clock next day, and all the members of the panel helped out with the chores such as putting out the corner flags, sweeping the car park and cleaning out the dressing rooms.

Paddy was a bit hassled with the final preparations, but the rest of the committee soon arrived and took over the donkey work and allowed him to concentrate on the team.

'That's been great work getting this off the ground Paddy,' said Mr McGrath, who turned out to be the chairman of the club. 'I see my gardeners are on the team – I hope they get to mow down the opposition today,' he chuckled.

After eleven o'clock the other clubs started arriving, and the club secretary, Simon, unveiled the tournament plan he and Paddy had come up with.

'This has to work like clockwork,' he explained to Alan and Eoin as they helped him stick the enormous fixture list to the wall.

'We have twenty clubs here, playing in four groups of five. That means you'll have three games today and one tomorrow morning – before the quarter-finals, semi-finals and final. We'll play on the two pitches, quarter of an hour each way, but even still we'll struggle to get all the games in. We might have to run a bit late tonight or start early tomorrow if we want to watch the All-Ireland semi-final.'

Simon had organised a panel of referees to help out, and ten minutes before noon they got the twenty teams together on the main pitch and explained how they wanted everything to run smoothly, with the next team on the sideline ready to start when the final whistle went in the previous game.

Eoin and his Ormondstown team-mates were a bit overwhelmed to see so many clubs descend on their little field. But not too overwhelmed, and they got into their stride quickly with a big win over one of the big town clubs.

Before their second game, Alan joined the team for a bottle of water on the sideline.

'I was thinking of checking out the teams you're playing later on,' he suggested. 'It would be good to work out their strengths and weaknesses.'

Eoin thanked him and off Alan went in search of their next opponents.

'He's so keen on sport isn't he,' Dylan said, 'even though he's pretty useless at it.'

'That's a bit mean,' said Eoin, 'but he'd admit himself that he's not really cut out for the action. He'll make a really good coach someday though.'

Eoin wandered around the ground and noticed Clonmel were playing on the back pitch. He lifted his hand to salute the player who he had chatted to when they met a few weeks earlier, and noticed that the hot-head, Cormac, was back in the team.

He went back to check the fixture list and was relieved that his club were in a different group to Clonmel, who were an excellent football side.

Just before their next game, Alan came back with a few tips – their opponents' defence was slow, and the keeper was afraid of diving – which Eoin filed away in the back of his head.

Vladis started at full-forward, and Eoin kept providing him with a steady stream of bullets to fire. When they changed over at half-time the home team were five points ahead so Paddy asked Vladis and Eoin to switch positions.

Eoin found it a weird place to play – in most team games he was at home around midfield, either in soccer or Gaelic, dictating and driving the game, just as he did from out-half in rugby. But full-forward meant he spent most of his time with his back to the goal looking back on all the action going on in the middle of the park.

He did get a couple of passes, and scored a point with one, but had already decided he didn't like playing there when Vladis came steaming through from the right with a clear shot on goal. He lifted his right boot and dropped the ball, the two objects meeting with a thud.

But Vlad had been moving at speed and a slight dip in the ground caused him to lean over a fraction just as he kicked the ball. The ball evaded the keeper, but was heading wide when Eoin came charging in from the left and stuck his right boot out. His action did enough to divert the ball and it ended in the back of the net.

'You've Broganed them,' cheered Alan from behind the goal where he had been watching the game.

'I don't even know what that means,' said the old man standing beside Alan. 'But I do know what a goal looks like – and my grandson has just scored a cracking one!'

CHAPTER 26

'Thanks for coming along, Dixie,' said Eoin, as he walked off the field after the Gaels had notched up a second good win.

'You seemed to play well, I think,' said Dixie. 'Though to be honest I can't really tell.'

'Ah I wasn't too bad, but it's a team game, same as rugby. We all have to put our backs into it,' Eoin replied.

He took his grandfather over to the clubhouse where he showed him the fixture chart which Simon had been filling with results as the games finished.

'So, you're playing Grangemockler next – that's down near Kilkenny I think,' Dixie told him.

They studied the chart and reckoned that one more win would get the Gaels into the quarter-finals.

'It's amazing there's so many lads here from all over the county,' Dixie told him. 'Where are they all staying?'

'Oh, yeah, well we each have to take two lads in, and

most of the club members are taking two as well. If we had to pay for a hotel for everyone that would cost way too much.'

'Good idea,' said Dixie. 'I hope you get two nice lads now!'

Eoin enjoyed watching the different games, but he rejoined his team-mates for a warm-up before their final match of the day.

'Keep an eye on their big midfielder,' Alan warned them. 'He has a huge kick on him – he scored two points from nearly half-way in their last match.'

Eoin was back on the half-forward line, but went back to help out with ensuring the midfielder didn't get much ball. Grangemockler were a good side for such a small village and it was the Gaels' hardest match so far.

'That lad's a monster,' said Dylan as they sucked on their oranges at half-time. 'I'm glad I'm not marking him.'

Eoin kicked a couple of points from frees in the second half and the Gaels led by one with time running out. As fate would have it, the ball fell to their opponents' midfield giant who noticed the referee was about to blow for full-time. He launched one last kick from the middle of the field and watched it soar high over the crossbar.

'That's a draw so,' announced the ref after he had blown on his whistle, 'and the first of the day too.'

The Gaels match was one of the last to be played, so Eoin and his team-mates had a short meeting before they went into the main hall where all the teams were gathered. They all mixed well together and enjoyed the soft drinks and snacks that the club had provided for them.

Paddy then made a short speech thanking everyone for coming and lots of others for helping with the organisation of the weekend. Simon then got up on stage to tell them that they all needed to find out where they would be staying that night. He directed them to a big chart on the wall and asked them first to match up with any players who were present. All the others would be brought to meet the members who had offered to put them up.

Eoin went down to check out who would be his guests and was delighted to see they were two of the boys from Grangemockler.

'Dan and Michael?' he asked their coach, who pointed out the boys. They were brothers – Dan was the giant midfielder and Michael the corner-back.

They chatted for a few minutes before they were joined by Dylan, who didn't look happy.

'What's up Dyl?' asked Eoin.

'Did you see who I got,' he asked, pointing at the chart.

'You got two lads from Clonmel,' said Eoin.

'Yeah, and one of them is Cormac – that psycho who was sent off after we got into that scrap.'

CHAPTER 27

Dylan found Cormac – and his pal Pat – and introduced himself as their one-night-only landlord. Cormac's face fell at first, but then laughed.

'I wonder did our two coaches do that on purpose to throw us together?' he suggested.

'Well, we better get on with it so,' said Dylan, extending his hand for Cormac to shake. 'Welcome to Ormondstown.'

Eoin, Alan and the brothers joined them and Dylan suggested a trip to Superburgers for a quick bite.

'My mam is out at work so we'll have to get our own dinner – but don't worry, you're my guest,' he told Cormac and Pat.

Eoin and his visitors bade them farewell, keen to get home to where Mrs Madden had made them a nice roast dinner.

They walked through the town, Eoin pointing out

the various sights he thought they might be interested in. The boys were shy, though, and didn't make much conversation. Eoin was relieved when they reached home and he could let his mother take over as host.

She was very welcoming, plying them with orange juice and showing them where they would be sleeping that night. She also conducted an interrogation of them of which a police detective would have been proud.

'So – you're actually twins,' she said. 'And your dad is a farmer. No wonder you're so big and strong.'

'And Michael is the best at school, but Dan is the best footballer,' she added.

'Well you are very welcome to our home, lads. I don't know if you want to go out later, but you would be welcome to sit in and watch the big movie too.'

'That would be very nice, Mrs Madden,' said Michael. 'We're a bit tired after the football so I don't think we'll head out, if that's OK, Eoin.'

'Grand, no problem,' said Eoin. 'I enjoy a good movie myself, though I might go for a bit of a run afterwards if it's not raining.'

After dinner, the boys settled in with the Madden family to watch television. Alan decided to do more Gaelic study on YouTube so he disappeared upstairs. Eoin hated being stuck indoors and thought the film was boring, but he also knew it would be wrong to leave the Grangemockler boys alone with his parents.

Once the film ended, the visitors thanked their hosts and headed to the spare bedroom. Eoin stood up and stretched and announced he was off on a run – he called up the stairs to ask Alan if he would like to join him, but his friend was happy where he was.

'I'm doing important work here, Eoin,' Alan told him. 'You'll thank me for this tomorrow night.'

Eoin slipped out the front door and worked out which route he would take on his run. He decided to head down past his grandfather's house – it was too late to call in but he'd check if there were any troublemakers hanging around.

All was peaceful around Dixie's house so he jogged past it towards the Lubov Mansion, a huge spooky house that had been empty for decades and was in a bad state of repair. Eoin had once had an adventure that centred on the house and the ghost of an old Russian prince that once upon a time played rugby for England.

He smiled as he thought of Alex Obolensky and was so distracted that he didn't see that Brian Hanrahan had stepped out of the shadows into his path.

'Heyyyy!!' said Eoin as he pulled up just in time. 'I know I can't bump you or knock you over, but you really should be careful about getting in people's way.'

Brian grinned at his pal. 'I'm sorry Eoin, I don't have huge control over where and when I appear – but I'll try harder next time.'

Eoin laughed. 'Sorry, it's just that you gave me a bit of a fright. What has you back in these parts?'

Brian shrugged his shoulders. 'I haven't a clue – I was hoping you might be able to tell me. And I tell you something, there's another ghost knocking around. I bumped into that fellow we met up in Croke Park earlier in the year – the lad Hogan who was shot dead there during a Gaelic match.'

Eoin nodded as he remembered walking out on to the pitch after Ireland had won a rugby match there, and meeting the ghost of the Tipperary corner-back who had died on that pitch back in 1920.

'There's something in the air, Eoin, be careful,' said Brian, before he disappeared, leaving Eoin to run home a little faster than he had run getting there.

CHAPTER 28

Next morning, they all got up early and Mrs Madden served them up a huge cooked breakfast.

'We'll have to leave about ten past nine,' Eoin told his dad. 'Do you mind giving us a spin?'

Eoin's dad agreed and they all tucked into plates piled high with eggs and bacon.

The twins were still very quiet, but Alan filled the silence by rabbiting on about how he was a huge fan of Gaelic football and comparing the styles of Kerry and Mayo teams.

Eoin's dad talked to the twins about their home village in the south east of the county.

'That's where that fellow Michael Hogan was from, isn't it?' he asked. 'You know, the lad they named the Hogan Stand after…'

Dan looked at Michael, who smiled at Mr Madden.

'It is indeed,' he replied. 'He was some sort of ancestor

of ours – that's who I'm named after. I'm Michael Hogan too.'

Eoin's jaw dropped and a piece of sausage fell out on to the plate. He remembered the conversation with Brian from the night before and realised that it was no coincidence that the Croke Park ghost had arrived in Ormondstown.

'I've met him…' Eoin started, 'I mean… I've heard and read about him. We had a class in school on Bloody Sunday 1920. It was very sad.'

'It was,' said Michael, 'but it was a long time ago now, and anyone that knew anyone there that day is long dead themselves.'

The boys finished up their meals and put their cups and plates in the dishwasher before going back to their rooms to collect their kitbags.

'That was a close one, Eoin,' Alan said when they were alone. 'You nearly gave it away about the ghost.'

'I know!' said Eoin, 'And the weird thing is that I met Brian last night when I was out for that run. And he told me that the Michael Hogan ghost was around the place too.'

Alan's eyes bulged. 'That IS very weird. I'm really sorry I didn't go out now – I'd love to see Brian again.'

Alan was one of very few people who were able to

see and talk to Brian, a gift that he had earned by being a good friend to Eoin.

There was no more talk of the old Michael Hogan during the car journey down to the Gaels. Eoin's dad wished all his passengers luck, and begged the Hogan boys' forgiveness that he wanted Ormondstown to win more.

Once they reached the ground the visiting boys thanked Mr Madden again and headed off to find their own team-mates.

Alan and Eoin went over to see Simon who seemed happy with the way the tournament was going.

'Did you notice we were only two minutes late finishing last night,' the club secretary said with a grin. 'It went like clockwork. Now today will be a different story with the knockout rounds and everyone stopping to watch Tipp at half past three.'

Eoin went into the dressing rooms and quickly changed into his Gaels shirt and shorts. He thought about all the great rugby shirts he'd worn – from the British and Irish Lion cubs, to Ireland, to Leinster, to his school one. But the Gaels one was special too, because it was the shirt that showed he represented his hometown, the place where all the people he loved in the world lived.

He pulled his socks on quickly and tied the laces on his boots just as Paddy called into the dressing room.

'You're last as usual Madden,' he said with a grin.

'Really? Dylan's always last,' he replied.

'Not today. He's been down since half past eight playing kickabout with his new pals.'

Eoin went outside to see Dylan down the back pitch kicking a ball around with Isaac, Pat and Cormac.

'Hey there Eoin, come and join in,' roared Dylan, 'we're having great crack with these Clonmel lads.'

Eoin just shook his head in disbelief, happy that Dylan had made up with a player that looked ready to kill him just a few weeks before. Now they looked like best friends forever.

'Ah, the power of sport,' he muttered to himself before he jogged over to join them.

CHAPTER 29

Paddy told them that he was delighted that they had played so well the day before and if they kept that up they'd be keeping the trophy the club had put up for the competition.

'I don't want to take any game for granted, but this team we are playing next are very weak – they lost all their games yesterday. So I'm going to give a few lads a start who haven't had a run so far,' he told them.

Eoin was glad Paddy had done that. He'd played on teams before where the coach just wanted to win every game and didn't care whether some boys got to play or not. That usually meant those boys soon lost interest and gave up the sport.

Paddy's attitude would ensure boys and girls would stay playing their games as long as they were enjoying it, which could only be good for the club.

And Paddy was right about the opposition, and that

meant he didn't have to take off the weaker players who were delighted to get a whole game and to play their part in winning the match – and getting Ormondstown into the quarter-finals.

Alan went off to find out the position in the other groups so he could check on their possible next opponents, while Eoin chatted with Dylan.

'What did you get up to last night?' he asked his pal.

'Not much,' Dylan replied. 'I brought the lads up the town for a wander and we nearly bumped into Rocky and his boys. They crossed over the street when they saw us coming! I was secretly hoping they might try something on so I could unleash my lethal weapon Cormac on them.'

'Ha, that would have been funny,' Eoin said. 'I wonder have they discovered their secret stash has been rumbled.'

'I expect they must have – I wonder did the guards stake it out. I'd say Rocky's dad would have loved to have been given that job to do.'

Alan returned with the not-so-good news that they were playing Clonmel in the quarter-final.

'Oh well, I suppose we can sit back and watch the All-Ireland semi without having to worry about playing a game afterwards,' sighed Dylan.

'Ah don't be like that Dyl, sure even I was able to score against them when we played them – this will be a shorter game so we might give them a fright. And Cormac won't want to smack you now that you are besties.'

Eoin turned out to be right about that. Maybe Dylan had managed to turn Cormac into a nicer kid, or maybe his coach had threatened him with a life ban if he got up to his old tricks – one way or the other the carrot and stick treatment made Cormac focus on trying to play football rather than look for fights.

But Ormondstown had been working hard since their first football practice a few weeks before and had improved enormously. Their new skill and aware-ness surprised Clonmel, and they were further shocked when Dylan managed to waltz past Cormac to score two goals in the first half.

'Will you tackle him, hit him hard,' shouted the Clon-mel captain at his full back, who just shrugged in reply.

With Vladis also knocking the ball over from all angles, the Gaels led by 2-7 to 0-6 at half-time, a healthy lead.

Eoin patted Dylan on the head at the break and joked about how he had Cormac in his pocket now.

The Clonmel boys tried to stoke their team-mate up, but to no avail as he never once lost his temper in the second half either. It seemed to deflate his side, and they never got within two scores of the Gaels for the rest of the game.

'That's some result,' said Alan as he cheered them off the field. 'You're playing Templederry in the semi – they've a couple of good players, but are lucky to have got this far.'

Eoin marvelled at how quickly Alan had turned himself into an expert on juvenile football in Tipperary.

'Cheers, Alan, any idea what the Templederry coach had for his breakfast this morning though?'

Alan stopped and scratched his chin, before he realised Eoin was winding him up. He replied: 'Bowl of muesli and a fried egg,' before throwing an empty water bottle at his friend.

CHAPTER 30

There was very little time between the quarter-final and semi-final, so little that neither side needed much of a warm-up.

Eoin had gone to primary school with two of the Templederry defenders and they swopped memories while play was up the other end.

It wasn't up the other end for long however, as Alan's scouting ensured the Gaels kept the ball away from the star players on the opposition and were able to quickly take control of the game.

Once Vladis scored a goal from a free that dipped under the cross bar the heart seemed to go from Templederry. Eoin was enjoying taking frees and never missed one as his team romped to victory by eleven points.

Paddy came rushing onto the pitch, beaming with pride at his young charges.

'That was fantastic,' he said. 'You never gave them a

chance. I'm so proud of ye. Now, let's get into the hall and get ourselves a good seat to watch this match, and we can think about the final afterwards,' he added.

As Eoin walked off the field he was greeted by his parents, and Dixie, who were just as delighted at the result.

'I never knew we had a Gaelic star in our family,' said his mother. 'My father would have been so proud of you... Not that he wouldn't have been proud of your achievements in rugby too, of course,' she added, hastily.

'Well done, son,' said his dad, 'Dixie and I were just saying how your rugby goal-kicking has been very useful in this competition.'

Eoin smiled back at them. 'Yeah, there's been a few things in both sports I've been able to switch between. I better go now though – the lads mightn't keep me a seat for the Tipp match.'

Eoin need not have worried as Isaac had ensured no one took the chair reserved for him.

With only two teams left in the competition, a lot of the other kids were guzzling soft drinks and munching on crisps, but Paddy would not allow the Gaels near the tuck shop.

'Here, the club has organised some healthy drinks for you,' he said, handing them each a bottle of water and carton of apple juice, as well as a banana and a granola bar.

'Chew slowly and make the snacks last the first half of the Tipp match at least. We need you on top form for the final.'

Eoin settled down and started watching the match. He rarely got a chance to watch much hurling but always tried to catch his native county when they were in the big games.

They were playing Galway; Croke Park seemed to be almost full for one of the biggest games of the year.

Eoin had played in front of big crowds himself, but never as many as that – he read somewhere that Croker was the biggest stadium in Europe. He wondered whether he would ever get a chance to play there in front of a full house.

From what Isaac and Vladis had told him, Tipperary had unearthed some excellent young players and were strong favourites to win. All the Ormondstown supporters were cheering on Pat Nugent, their local hero, but lots of the other clubs present had players on the county panel.

It all made for an exciting atmosphere as every time a Tipp player touched the sliotar there was a huge cheer from one pocket of spectators. The Templederry lads made the loudest cheer when their local hero, John Young, scored a brilliant goal.

But every time a point was taken the whole room erupted. And there were plenty of those moments, as Tipperary romped to a comfortable victory.

As the cheers for the full-time whistle echoed around the hall, secretary Simon stepped on to the stage and took the microphone.

'Well, that was a fantastic game, and a better result, wasn't it?' he asked.

After more cheers he said he had an important announcement to make.

'Before this game even took place, when we didn't know whether Tipp would be in the final or not, I had a chat with the chairman of the county board.

'And he told me to tell you that – if Tipp won – he would be providing twenty tickets for the All-Ireland final as a prize for the winning team in today's competition,' Simon revealed.

There were loud cheers around the hall, although some of the teams who had been already knocked out were now even more disappointed.

As Eoin looked across at the long faces on the Clonmel boys, he realised he didn't know who they would be playing in the final. He asked Alan, who looked at him as if he had two heads.

'Do you really not know?' he asked. 'It's going to be a cracker – we're playing that team we drew against already; we're playing Grangemockler.'

CHAPTER 31

Eoin's mouth opened wide in surprise. He hadn't bothered watching how the rest of the competition had been going, but was happy for the Hogan twins that they had reached the final too.

He waited patiently as the crowd made their way out of the hall, but as soon as he exited he ran around to the back pitch where his team-mates were already starting to do their warm-up stretches.

Having played Grangemockler already, there weren't any major new coaching secrets for Alan to report, although he passed on that he had noticed that their goalkeeper was a little weaker on his left side.

As they waited for the referee to throw the ball in, Eoin chatted away to Michael.

'Will you be going to Croke Park for the final even after you lose today?' he teased him.

'Ah sure we'll hardly need those twenty tickets –

there's hardly twenty lads live in our village anyway!' replied Michael. 'I might go twice.'

Play started and it was clear once more that Grange would be getting the ball to Dan as often as possible. His ability to kick the ball over the bar from almost any distance soon got the scoreboard moving and when the half-time whistle sounded his team led by five points to three.

As they stood around listening to Paddy's team-talk at half time, Eoin's eye was caught by two figures standing close to the goalposts as the far end of the ground. One was wearing a black, red and yellow hooped jersey, the other a white one with a green hoop that was the Tipperary jersey a century before.

'There's Brian,' he whispered to Dylan, 'and the other lad is the ghost I met in Croke Park.'

'That's a bit weird,' he replied. 'I can see Brian now you mention it, but I can't see the other lad. Wonder what they're doing here?'

Eoin wondered too, but supposed the ghost of Michael Hogan might be keeping an eye on his young descendants.

Paddy asked the team did they have anything they wanted to say, so Eoin mentioned that he was a bit frustrated that he had been unable to receive much ball.

He suggested that he move back to midfield to mark Dan. Paddy nodded – he trusted Eoin's opinion and was delighted he was willing to take on the best of their opponents.

Dan was a bit surprised at the move and seemed a little rattled when Eoin went in hard when the ball came next to him. The ball broke loose and Eamonn collected it and fed it up to Dylan who took a nice point.

'I enjoyed that,' said Eoin to Dan, who grimaced.

'That was nearly a rugby tackle,' his opponent complained.

'You mustn't watch much rugby if you think that,' Eoin grinned back.

The Ormondstown kickout came towards Dan once again, and again Eoin leapt to contest it. Dan was used to having things his own way in midfield and again backed away as Eoin snatched the ball from the air. As Eoin fell he checked his options and decided he wanted some glory for himself.

So off he set, remembering a brilliant goal he had seen in the All-Ireland the previous year. He raced through the gap between the half-backs and rounded the corner back. With Alan's advice flashing across his brain, he dropped the ball onto his foot and drove it hard and low to the goalkeeper's left.

He made a decent enough attempt to get down to it but even though he got his fingers to the ball the power of the shot was enough to break through them and into the corner of the net.

Eoin turned and took a little skip and punched the air. He was amazed at the roar that came from the crowd – it looked like half the town had come down to the club once the word had got around that the local boys were in the final.

He gathered himself quickly however and resumed his position. Dan won the next couple of balls and drew the sides level once more. As the referee's watch ticked on the atmosphere became more and more tense.

There was very little time left when a Grange forward took advantage of a slip by Matthew and was suddenly clear on goal with only the goalkeeper to beat. Isaac came rushing out as he saw the forward shape to take the point. The Gaels keeper charged forward and threw himself at him with his arms in the air and managed to block the score, earning him a huge cheer.

The loose ball fell to a Gaels defender who picked out Eoin with a perfect pass, and he hand-passed it on quickly to Vladis.

Dylan ran quickly upfield, waving his arms for a pass. Vlad looked up with half a mind to shoot before he opted to play it through to his team-mate.

Dylan had managed to evade his marker and was suddenly free on his own. With a quick sidestep he left the goalie on the grass and punched the ball into the empty net.

The sound of the referee's whistle to end the game was almost lost in the eruption of noise that greeted Dylan's winning goal. The rest of the panel raced on to the field to join the celebrations, and the locals cheered the young heroes who had brought glory to their club – and twenty priceless pieces of card with the words 'All Ireland hurling final ticket' printed on them.

CHAPTER 32

Eoin hugged Dylan as their families gathered around and slapped them on the back for the crucial roles they had played in the victory.

Eoin introduced Dylan's mum and sister to his grandad, and they chatted away as the boys went off to join their team-mates' celebrations.

Paddy was overjoyed and was delighted that so many of the local supporters had come out for the youngsters' match.

'We'll have to keep the football going here now,' he told Simon. 'Not that we'll slacken off the hurling of course.'

'And we'll have to organise an extra bus up to Dublin for the final too,' smiled Simon. 'There won't be a bus to be had in the county that day.'

The celebrations went on for a couple of hours but the Blooming Magic four decided to leave a little early and meet up in Eoin's house after dinner.

'Paddy paid me for the work on Friday,' Dylan reported to his work colleagues. 'He wouldn't hear anything about a discount and insisted we take the full amount – there's thirty euro each here,' he told them, taking a wad of bank notes out of his pocket.

'We've made a serious amount of money this week,' said Isaac.

'Over a hundred each,' said Alan.

'Not bad for a lad supposed to be on his holidays,' laughed Eoin.

'Will we keep it up for the last couple of weeks of the summer?' asked Dylan.

The boys all agreed they would, although they said they might cut back the work they would accept to one job a day and give themselves a Friday off – as well as weekends.

After the company meeting was over, they decided to go down the town.

'We're local heroes now, lads, we should be milking the love,' said Dylan with a grin.

They found they did get a few more stares and pointed fingers, but there was no discount in the sweetshop or free milk shakes in Superburgers.

As they sat on the park bench outside the Castle, Isaac wondered was sporting fame all it was cracked up to be.

'I don't know,' agreed Eoin. 'I'd say it gets to be a pain in the neck being stopped everywhere you go for selfies and autographs.' Eoin had a small taste of such attention after he became a schools rugby star at Castlerock College.

'Here's some attention we don't need,' muttered Isaac, as he spotted a small group of youths walking towards them.

Rocky and his gang paused once they realised who was sitting on the bench, but they didn't cross the road this time.

'Howya, Madden,' called Rocky. 'Heard ye won the football down the club. Stupid sport.'

'Cheers, Rocky,' Eoin answered him. 'You could be right, but it's nice to be good at something, isn't it?'

Rocky scowled. 'Did you lot hear anything about what happened to our hideout?' he asked.

'No, what happened to it?' enquired Dylan.

'It was emptied by the guards,' he answered. 'They say they got a tip off from someone from Sligo with a stupid American accent and an even stupider name.'

'Wasn't me so,' said Dylan. 'Nothing stupid about my

name.'

'Well if you hear, let me know, I'll be going out with a blaze of glory in this town and that's one score I want to settle,' Rocky added, before his band trudged on.

'What did he mean by a blaze of glory?' Eoin asked, once they were out of earshot.

'Did you not hear?' Isaac said. 'The Garda sergeant found out that Rocky was behind all the robberies and suggested to his father that he ask for a transfer. He's been moved to Dublin and they're leaving this week.'

'His father is lucky to be keeping his job, I'd say,' said Dylan. 'But no-one in Ormondstown will be mourning Rocky's departure.'

CHAPTER 33

The boys spent the next few days doing a few gardens and just generally rambling the roads and fields around Ormondstown. Alan and Eoin paid a visit to the old ruined Lubov Mansion, but there was no sign of any ghosts, and the doors and windows had been securely fastened to stop anyone breaking in.

They weren't afraid of Rocky and his gang anymore, but decided to keep clear of him after his threat. They played a bit of hurling too, everyone now keen to copy their county heroes as the buzz about the All-Ireland final increased.

'We'll have a ticket for Alan too for Croke Park,' Paddy told Eoin next time they met at the Gaels grounds. 'Some of his advice was very useful indeed. I hope he keeps up the coaching, whatever sport he gets into.'

After hurling they collected the mowers from Dixie's shed and went over to a house on the edge of town.

The owner had rung Dylan the previous evening to see could he cut the grass in his very large garden.

The boys had been surprised at just how large the area they had to cut was, but with two mowers on the go they expected it wouldn't take more than an hour or two. Dylan and Eoin sat on the patio while the other two did the first shift out the front.

'I think that Rocky lad lives around here,' Dylan started.

'Hopefully he keeps out of our way before he leaves town,' said Eoin.

They discussed their plans for the new school year and were happy to realise that they would be starting back at Castlerock the day after the All-Ireland final, meaning they would face just one long drive up to Dublin.

'It would be great to get a bit of GAA going up in the school, wouldn't it?' suggested Dylan. 'I know they're mad about the rugby, but playing a couple of different sports is really good for giving you new ideas and practising new skills, isn't it?'

Eoin agreed with him. 'And I'd say a few of the Dublin lads in school would be mad keen to try it now that they're the world champions at Gaelic.'

As they were chatting, Isaac popped his head around the corner.

'Sorry to disturb you, boys, but I've just noticed a removals van has pulled up across the road – and that Garda Ryan opened the door. The one who's Rocky's dad…'

Eoin and Dylan followed them around to the front just in time to see the removal men start to carry some armchairs into the van. The rest of the family joined in, with the father and mother bringing a table out to the garden. Rocky followed them, carrying with him a box of plates.

As he lifted the box into the van he glanced across to where the Blooming Magicians were standing, and gave them a frown. As he turned back to the house he stared at the mowers and waved his fist across at them.

'Oh dear, I think he's just realised where we got our equipment from,' said Alan with a chuckle.

'We better be careful now,' said Eoin, 'he could be dangerous now he has nothing to lose.'

The boys spent the rest of the afternoon finishing off mowing the enormous garden and were delighted to be paid with a bonus by the happy owner.

'I think I'll retire from the Bloomers,' Eoin announced as they walked home from the job.

'What?' asked a surprised Dylan.

'Ah, I'm enjoying the crack, but to be honest I need a

rest before we get back to school. We only have a couple of bookings for next week and I'm sure you can handle them.'

'And what about you, Alan?' asked Isaac.

'Well… Eoin and I hadn't discussed it, but I wouldn't mind a break too and I have to head back to see my folks on Wednesday anyway,' he replied.

Dylan looked a bit put out by their resignations, but when Isaac pointed out there was now a two-way cut on takings he cheered up a bit.

'Sorry, Dyl, hope you forgive me,' said Eoin as they arrived at Dylan's house.

'Yeah no worries, pal,' he replied. 'It's just things are a bit tight here now that Mam has lost one of her jobs. I have only one week more earning to be done down here before we head up to Dublin.'

CHAPTER 34

The boys enjoyed their last weekend together in Ormondstown, playing – and winning – a hurling challenge against Toomevara and exploring the forest down by the lake.

Eoin wondered how much longer his summers would be so carefree, and reckoned he would have to get a proper summer job next year – unless there was some big rugby tour that he didn't know about of course.

He hung around the house on Monday morning, guilty that he wasn't out working with Isaac and Dylan, but glad to have to time to chat to his mam and Alan.

Without the football project Alan seemed a bit aimless, and Eoin found him packing his bag that evening.

'You off early, Al?' he asked.

'Nah, just a bit bored,' he admitted. 'It's been such a busy summer and now we have nothing to do I'm scrabbling around to find things to keep me interested.'

'Let's go down and find Dyl and see if he's on for a stroll?' suggested Eoin, to which Alan agreed without huge enthusiasm.

On the way to Dylan's house they were stopped by a couple of smaller kids keen to get the autograph of Ormondstown's newest football hero.

'Are you going to play for Tipp?' one of them asked Eoin.

He laughed, and thought about his answer. 'That would be great I suppose,' he replied. 'But my pal here is going to be the next manager of Dublin, so I might play for them instead.'

The youngsters looked shocked and ran off to spread the hot news.

Eoin knocked on the Coonans' door and smiled when Caoimhe opened it.

'Hiya Ki, is the brother in?' he asked.

'Come on down the back,' came the roar from inside, where Dylan was sitting eating his dinner.

'We finished the gardens late tonight,' he moaned, 'we were a bit short handed without you two.'

'Did you turn up at ten o'clock like you said?' asked Eoin.

'Well… no, it was more like half-eleven,' admitted Dylan.

'So that's why you finished at seven o'clock so,' said Eoin, 'don't go blaming us on you not having enough time for a job.'

Dylan looked a bit grumpy at this, but had no answer for his friend.

'Ah, sorry for getting on your case. My mam wasn't here to wake me up – she's desperately looking for a new job. I brought more money into the house last week than her,' he sighed. 'I don't know what she's going to do when I go back to school.'

Eoin apologised for being so critical, and they shared a hug.

After a while Eoin suggested they go down to visit Dixie, and they found the old man trimming his rose bushes out the front.

'Easy now, Dixie,' Dylan started. 'That's a job for professional gardeners. Do you want us down for a few hours before we go back to school?'

Dixie chuckled at Dylan's cheek.

'No, I think my rose trimming will have to be done on an amateur basis this year. I came out here because the indoors is getting me down to be honest. I was hoping someone would come along for a chat. Can I get you a cup of tea?'

Eoin and the boys were happy to join Dixie, who dug

out his secret stash of their favourite chocolate biscuits.

'Please excuse the mess again,' he said. 'I'm finding it harder and harder to keep the place clean and tidy.'

Alan picked up the discarded newspapers and put them in a neat pile in the kitchen, while Eoin made a start on washing the dishes. Dylan took the sacks of groceries from inside the front door and stacked their contents in the fridge and the kitchen cupboards.

'Oh gosh, I forgot about the milk,' Dixie said. 'I popped out for a few things before tea, but I was so exhausted carrying the bags that I dropped them inside the door there and came in here to sit down.'

'Why don't you give me a shout when you want any messages, Grandad? I'd be delighted to be able to help out,' said Eoin.

'Thank you, thank you,' said Dixie, 'but I do enjoy going out and chatting to the girls in the shops. I suppose if it's raining I could give you a call though,' he added, with a grin.

CHAPTER 35

On Wednesday it was time for Alan to go home. It was a nice morning so Eoin suggested they walk down to get the bus.

'Our "jog every night" idea didn't really go to plan, did it?' Eoin said as they lugged the suitcases along. 'That said, you're a good bit fitter than you were when you got here. We'll have to get that going again when we get back to school.'

Eoin wasn't meeting Paddy to collect the tickets until Friday night so he and Alan made arrangements to meet back at Castlerock and to travel up to Croke Park with Dylan on Sunday morning.

As Alan stepped on board the bus a foil packet fell out of his pocket.

Eoin picked it up. 'What's this Al?' he asked with a grin.

'You know your mother,' he replied, 'she forced me to

take a couple of slices of apple tart for the journey.'

'Forced?' said Eoin, 'Right so, extra laps of the pitch in Castlerock on Monday night!'

They made their farewells and Eoin strolled back through the village humming to himself.

He had an idea, and texted Dylan to share it with him.

'Go 4 it,' came his reply. 'I'll sort this end.'

Eoin called into the newsagent and bought a history magazine for Dixie before he walked out to his cottage.

'Hi, Grandad, how are you today?' he asked, handing him the present.

'Oh… that's very thoughtful of you Eoin, thank you,' the old man said with a smile.

'Can I come in?' he asked, 'I have something I want to suggest to you.'

Dixie ushered Eoin inside and put the kettle on.

'You know the way you were saying you were finding it hard to keep the house clean?' his grandson asked. 'Well I wonder would you like to get someone in to help you. It wouldn't cost you very much and the place would be spick and span – and she would be great to have a chat with too.'

'That sounds like a very good idea young Eoin – and

it also sounds like you have someone in mind for me....'

Eoin heard the garden gate opening and went out to open the door and bring in the visitors.

'Oh, hello Dylan,' said Dixie. 'And this is your mother who I met down at the Gaels. Can I get you a cup of tea?'

'Mrs Coonan is the person I was talking about coming to give you a hand around the house,' said Dylan.

'Ah, well that would be very nice,' said Dixie, as he brought in the teapot.

'Maybe we should leave you two on your own to discuss how this would work,' suggested Eoin. 'And we'll see you later.'

Outside, Dylan gave a huge grin.

'That was a brilliant idea, Eoin,' he said. 'She's desperate for work and this would be a good start for her. Dixie is such a nice old codger too, she'll enjoy the chats with him.'

'He's got loads of pals, too,' Eoin said. 'If it works well he'll spread the word among them – it'll be like Blooming Magic, she could get loads of jobs out of it.'

'Yeah... and she could call it Brooming Magic too.'

CHAPTER 36

Eoin arrived back in Castlerock on Saturday night. His dad had driven him up with Dylan and they all had a bit of fun swopping stories about their summer mischief.

Eoin's dad told him he was delighted with the plan for Dixie to get some help around the house and was relieved to have someone else to keep an eye on the old man.

When they got to school the boys made their farewells and lugged their suitcases, kitbags and schoolbags into the hallway. Dylan complained that it was going to be a pain having to carry them all the way up to the second floor where the fourth-year dormitories were situated. Eoin winked at Dylan and said, 'Just wait a minute.'

Sure enough, a gaggle of second year students came down the corridor and pointed at Eoin.

'Hey Eoin, had you a good summer?' said one.

'We saw you on TV playing for the Lions,' said another.

'Do you want a hand carrying your bags up?' asked a third.

'Thanks lads, that would be great,' said Eoin, winking at Dylan.

The youngsters helped them lift the stuff upstairs and were rewarded with a selfie with their hero.

'Thanks Eoin,' they called as they strolled back down the corridor while the older boys let themselves into their new home.

'Only three beds this year,' Dylan noted. 'Any idea when Alan is arriving?'

'He'll be here in the morning before we head to the final. I must confess I can't wait. Haven't been as buzzed about a game I'm not playing in for ages.'

The boys tossed a coin for choice of beds before they unpacked all their clothes and books. Once their chores were done they headed down to the canteen to see if they could get some dinner.

The full kitchen staff weren't starting until school commenced on Monday, but the boys were able to get some beans on toast and a glass of milk from the one lady who was working there.

'Don't tell anyone I gave you that,' she winked at them. 'Or everyone will be down looking to be fed. But

I couldn't say no to the biggest schools rugby star in the country.'

Eoin smiled and thanked her, and went to sit down in a quiet corner with Dylan.

'I think I'll stick close to you this term,' Dylan said. 'There's plenty of perks in being Eoin Madden's plus one.'

Dylan had been working on the last of the Blooming Magic jobs right up to leaving for Dublin, so he was too tired to join Eoin when he suggested going for a jog after dinner.

Eoin had a particular circuit of the school grounds he followed every time, finishing in a secluded wooded area through which a stream ran, down beside one of the outside walls.

He did two full laps of Castlerock before he decided to take a break, ducking through the bushes and trees till he reached The Rock, a giant stone where he often met Brian – and other ghosts.

He leaned up against The Rock and closed his eyes, taking a rest after running a hard second lap.

'Are you asleep, young man?' came a familiar voice.

Eoin opened his eyes to see Brian standing in front of him with a worried look on his face.

'No, just resting my eyes,' Eoin replied. 'What's up

with you?'

'I don't know, Eoin,' Brian answered. 'I wasn't sure why I suddenly turned up in Clonmel and Ormond-stown either, and now with Mick Hogan knocking around I'm concerned that you're about to have one of your adventures.'

Eoin winced. 'I'm going to Croke Park tomorrow, for the hurling final. Do you think it has anything to do with that?'

Brian stroked his chin. 'I supposed it could have,' he said. 'But there will be eighty thousand people there. How are we supposed to keep track of you?'

'I don't know. There's nothing that I can think of that might cause trouble,' Eoin replied.

'I expect Mick will turn up later,' said Brian. 'Maybe he will have some ideas. Meanwhile, keep your wits about you and keep safe.'

CHAPTER 37

Next morning Eoin went for another quick lap of the grounds, but there were no ghosts to be seen around The Rock, or anywhere else.

As he jogged back up the steps he bumped into Mr Finn, an old team-mate of Dixie, who had been a teacher in Castlerock for his whole career. He was retired now, but regularly come back to help out in the school to which he had dedicated his life.

'Ah Eoin, good to see you again,' the old teacher said. 'And I hope my pal Richard is keeping well?'

'He's not too bad, Mr Finn,' replied Eoin. 'He's still getting out every day for a walk and watching plenty of horse racing. He even watched a bit of Gaelic football and hurling this summer.'

'Ah, of course, he now lives in Tipperary and they are in the final of the hurling tomorrow – you see, I do keep up with the news,' said Mr Finn with a smile.

'Yes, and I was lucky enough to win a ticket for the final – Alan, Dylan and I are heading over there shortly.'

At that moment Alan came around the corner puffing as he lugged his bags into the school.

'Ah that was good timing Alan. I'm sure Master Madden here won't mind giving you a hand upstairs with that stuff. Now, have a good day at the match and I'll see you tomorrow.'

As Mr Finn walked off, Eoin looked all around him.

'There's never a junior when you really need one,' he sighed, as he lifted Alan's heaviest bag onto his shoulder and headed for the staircase.

Once Alan had settled in, the boys set off for the railway station where they caught a DART into the city centre. Dylan and Eoin wore Tipperary shirts and were surprised to see they weren't the only ones aboard wearing those colours. There were even a few wearing the green of Limerick.

'I love this journey into Dublin,' said Alan. 'Especially the seaside bit.'

'I prefer the bit when you go behind the stand at the Aviva Stadium,' said Eoin. 'It always brings me back to our days out on the pitch.'

'I agree,' said Dylan. 'It's cool that there's a train station right beside the ground too.'

'One thing I never understood about Croke Park was that they always talk about the Dublin fans standing at the Railway End. But the train tracks run at both ends,' said Alan.

The other two looked at Alan as if he had just grown a second nose, but they just sniggered and sighed.

'You need to stop thinking so much about the stupid stuff, Al,' said Dylan. 'There's a railway at the Railway End, and a railway and a canal at the other end, so they call that the Canal End.'

'But why don't they call it the Canal and Railway End?' asked Alan. 'It seems a bit unfair to the other railway line.'

Happily, the train was just pulling into Lansdowne Road so they managed to change the subject.

'There's still a lot of cranes and scaffolding around, isn't there,' said Alan. 'I wonder when they will be finished fixing it up?'

Eoin had become a bit of a hero earlier in the year when he spotted the stadium was in danger of collapse. His quick actions had averted a major tragedy.

'Hopefully in time for the schools senior cup final next year,' announced Dylan. 'I fancy getting my hands on that little beauty.'

They soon arrived at Connolly Station and left the train with almost all the other passengers. Eoin checked his pocket for the seventeenth time that morning to be sure he had not forgotten the tickets. They descended the escalator and joined the exodus of match goers on the last leg of their journey to Croke Park.

CHAPTER 38

The boys walked as quickly as they could. Even though their tickets were numbered and their seats guaranteed, they were keen to get there early and savour the full experience of All-Ireland final day.

They reached a gap in the rows of Georgian houses and spotted the huge modern stadium rising above them. They soon reached Russell Street and pushed their way through the crowds where men and women with carts and stalls called out what they had on sale such as 'pears and chocolate,' and 'hats, scarves and headbands'.

As they went to cross the bridge into Jones's Road, where the main entrance stood, Eoin's eye was caught by a strange sight. Up high to his right he saw a child sitting in the upper branches of a tree that was leaning against the end wall of the stadium. It was a young boy, wearing a jumper and short pants.

The boy turned towards him and looked Eoin straight

in the eye. Suddenly, Eoin heard a shot ring out and the boy winced. A dark patch appeared and grew on his shoulder, and the boy fell from the tree to a piece of ground between the canal and the railway line far below.

'Oh my God!' said Eoin. 'Did you see that?'

'See what?' said Alan.

'See that boy in the tree there – it looked like he was shot.'

'What tree?' asked Dylan. 'There's no tree there – just cement walls and those roundy staircases.'

'Come on, let's go, he looks like he needs help – if he even survived the fall.'

Eoin pushed his way through the crowds and looked over the railings down to where the boy lay. He vaulted them and let himself down gently to the grassy area.

He approached the boy and could see he looked no more than eleven or twelve years old and was wearing very strange, scruffy clothes and a battered pair of shoes.

The boy looked up at him, puzzled.

'Are you shot?' asked Eoin.

'I am,' said the boy. 'I'm Perry, Perry Robinson. Will you tell my da I've been shot?'

Eoin said he would, and looked up to the bridge to try to see where the boy's father might be, but when he turned back there was nothing on the grass but a clump of dandelions.

He looked around, and further along the outside wall of the ground another boy was sitting. He too turned his head to stare at Eoin, and again another shot rang out. The boy fell instantly, out of sight.

Eoin looked for a way down to reach the youngster but there was no way of doing so from where he stood.

A garda called out to him, saying he was trespassing and what he would do if he caught him.

'I have a match ticket,' Eoin replied, 'I just came down here for a look. I'm sorry.'

The garda was gone by the time he had scrambled back up. Eoin explained what he had seen to his pals.

'This is you seeing ghosts again, isn't it,' said Dylan.

Eoin nodded. 'It was terrible, I saw another lad being shot too – and they were both very young.'

The trio were rattled by the experience, especially Eoin, but he decided there was no point saying anything to a policeman and so they headed down Jones's Road towards the entrance marked on their ticket.

'You're shaking, Eoin,' said Alan. 'Do you want to stop for a drink or something?'

Eoin shook his head. 'I don't understand what's going on – it's like I'm seeing something that happened a long time ago, but in real time.'

'Is it that Bloody Sunday thing we learned about in school?' asked Dylan.

'I think so,' said Eoin.

The boys reached the entrance, which was just beside the elevated railway line. Suddenly, Eoin saw another youngster rush from inside the stadium and dash up one of the side streets. He pointed him out to his pals.

'Yeah, I can see him,' said Dylan.

'Me too!' said Alan.

The boy stopped for a second and looked over to where the three friends stood before turning to run away. At that instant he was cut down by a bullet that had ricocheted from the wall opposite him. He fell to the ground.

The trio ran over to him, pushing past the supporters on their way into the ground.

'You're Billy Scott, aren't you,' said Alan, remembering the name of the fourteen-year-old victim he had learned about in school.

Billy's eyes widened and he stared at these three mysterious strangers wearing clothes from the far future.

'Do I know you? Is that some sort of Tipperary jersey?' he asked, staring at the county crest.

'It is,' said Eoin.

'Are you one of the players?' he gasped, in obvious pain.

'No, no, it's just a replica shirt I bought online. It was fifty euro…'

Eoin realised that most of what he had just said would mean nothing to a boy born in 1906.

Billy closed his eyes and, soon after, he was gone.

CHAPTER 39

'That's unbelievable,' said Dylan, reeling with shock as he looked down to where Billy had lain moments before.

'I remembered his name,' said Alan, gasping. 'I think that was a bit weird for him.'

'That was the least of his worries,' Eoin pointed out.

The crowds of spectators were rushing past all the time, and some were irritated at the boys standing in the middle of the street.

'Get a move on,' one man snapped at them, so they sidled across to the footpath.

'What can we do?' asked Dylan.

'Nothing,' said Eoin. 'They're ghosts, long dead. We have just been allowed to be witnesses to the replaying of their last moments. If we said anything to the Garda they'd want us to go and get our heads examined.'

'You're right,' said Alan. 'Let's get inside and find our

seats and try to forget this. There's nothing we can do to help.'

As they walked back to towards the stadium Eoin stayed silent, thinking about how lucky he was to be born at a time and place where people weren't shot at in sports grounds.

The boys went through the turnstiles and took their seats high in the Hogan Stand. The excitement and good humour was gone however and the three just sat, mostly silently, while the match between the minor teams was played.

As throw-in time in the senior final approached, Eoin stood and suggested he go and pick up some drinks and popcorn.

'I'll give you a hand,' Dylan said, leaving Alan to mind their seats in case anyone tried to nick them.

The boys headed for the refreshment stalls behind the stand and bought three containers of soft drinks as well as some snacks. As they were walking back to retake their seats they bumped into a garda.

'Careful, lads,' he said, before stopping and staring at them.

'You're those kids from Ormondstown,' he said, his face darkening. 'You caused me an awful lot of trouble.'

'Your young fella caused all the trouble,' replied Dylan.

'Careful, son,' snarled Garda Ryan, 'I can make trouble for you too if you like.'

Eoin put his hand on Dylan's shoulder and guided him away from Rocky's father.

'That was stupid getting into a row with a guard,' he told him when they were out of sight of the policeman. 'You can't win those arguments and he could have seriously messed up our day – it would be our word against his and they would all take his side.'

Dylan nodded and they made for their seats just in time for the parade of the teams and the national anthem. By that time Paddy and the rest of the Gaels had arrived and Isaac greeted the rest of the Bloomers like they hadn't seen each other for weeks.

'How's the gardening going?' Eoin asked Isaac.

'Pretty good,' he replied. 'I've taken on two new assistants – my little brother and Caoimhe. They work a lot harder than Dylan and Alan!'

They settled into their seats and cheered all the Tipperary players' names when they were read by the announcer and gave a special roar when Pat Nugent's name was called out.

The people in the seats around them were amused by their antics and quite a few people in the rows in front turned around to see who was making all the noise.

Right down at the front, about twenty metres away, Eoin recognised a face, and gave Alan an elbow in the ribs to alert him too.

'Wow, that's Rocky,' his friend said. 'I wonder what he's doing here.'

'Well I suppose he is from Tipp so he's entitled to be here,' Dylan smirked. 'His father was out the back when we got the drinks too, shooting his mouth off about how we had ruined his life.'

The game started just then, and the boys soon forgot the earlier dramas. Limerick were a lot tougher than their semi-final opponents and they had a pair of brothers who were causing all sorts of problems. Killian O'Neill was playing a stormer in midfield, and his brother Ólan had scored a goal with his boot before Tipperary had even gathered themselves.

When the half-time whistle blew Eoin looked down to the Canal End to check the score – Tipp were five points behind – when he noticed a crowd of people running onto the field, most wearing flat caps and heavy overcoats.

'Do you see that?' Eoin asked Alan, who just shrugged and asked, 'Do I see what?'

Eoin pointed down to the field, but Alan said all he saw was a brass band and kids playing seven a side.

But Eoin could see a lot more than that – he could see hundreds of people rushing across the ground and disappearing into the stands, followed by men carrying rifles and pistols who were shooting at them.

Several people fell, and Eoin then noticed that some men wearing Tipperary shirts and shorts were lying face down on the ground.

'They're moving,' he whispered to Alan. 'Looks like they've taken cover and are trying to crawl away.'

Eoin watched with increasing horror as he saw one of the men flinch and put his hand down to his back. He recognised him as Mick Hogan, who he had first met on that same spot.

Another man rushed up to him and whispered something in his ear, before he too fell to the ground.

CHAPTER 40

'That's how it happened,' Eoin gasped as he watched the mayhem unfold. 'Poor Mick.'

He watched as another man appeared from out of the crowd, wearing a black, red and gold hooped jersey. He bent down and lifted up the lifeless body of Mick Hogan and carried him away in his arms past where the modern grandstands now stood

'Brian...' Eoin whispered to himself.

He was shaken by what he had seen, and tried to explain it to Alan, who was concerned at what it all might mean.

'The ghosts only come along when you're in trouble,' he said. 'And this seems to be the most extraordinary episode yet.'

Eoin nodded and tried to concentrate on the match, which had just restarted.

Happily, Tipperary seemed to be re-energised by what

their manager had told them during the break and came storming back in the second half. Nugent got the crowd to their feet with a brilliant solo which he finished off with a flourish.

'Go on, Nugget!' roared Dylan, 'we can win this you know.'

The boys became engrossed as Tipp slowly took control and a succession of long-distance points, mostly by Nugent and John Young, gave them a comfortable lead going into the last few minutes.

A high ball deep into the Tipp half fell nicely for Ólan O'Neill however, and as he broke past the defence he dropped the sliotar onto his lethal left foot and smashed it past the keeper.

'Hey ref, this is hurling, not football,' roared Dylan, 'that's unfair.'

'Don't be stupid Dylan, that's perfectly allowed,' said Alan. 'You would be better off giving Tipp a cheer – they're level now.'

Eoin confirmed the score on the giant screen and focused on the action on the field. Pat Nugent was drifting further up field and calling for the ball from his keeper.

The number one unleashed an enormous puck out and Nugent knew exactly where he needed to be to pluck it from the sky. He turned, and with one shimmy past a defender he arrowed the sliotar straight between the posts.

The Limerick goalkeeper barely had time to retrieve the ball before the referee gave two long blasts on his whistle.

'We're champions,' roared Dylan, as he hugged Isaac and Eoin in turn. Even Alan was doing a little jig.

'That was magic,' said Eoin. 'What a player The Nugget is.'

The Ormondstown group danced in their seats and roared their approval at the victory, cheering even louder when the Tipperary captain lifted the Liam MacCarthy Cup to the skies.

With everyone's eyes on the presentation, Eoin was distracted by the sudden reappearance of Brian and Mick standing right in front of him.

'Eoin, quick, to your right!' Brian said urgently.

Eoin turned to see the glistening flash of the sun reflecting off a penknife as the hand holding it moved towards Dylan's back.

Flanked by his ghostly friends, Eoin grabbed the wrist with his left hand and karate chopped down with his right, knocking the blade from the hand and causing the boy who had been holding it to scream in pain.

Dylan and Paddy turned around and were astonished to see the scene in front of them. Moving quickly, Paddy grabbed the culprit and sent Isaac off to find a policeman – 'Don't get the one at the food stand,' Eoin told him – while he checked that no harm had been done to the boys. Dylan hadn't even noticed he was in danger until it was all over.

Two gardaí arrived and took hold of the youngster who had wielded the knife, which they picked up carefully from the ground and put in a clear plastic bag.

A third guard joined them and his face fell when he saw who the perpetrator was.

'Oh Rocky, Rocky, what have you done,' moaned his father. 'You can't be doing things like that,' he added, before following the other gardaí as they led his son away.

Dylan thanked Eoin.

'How did you know I was in danger?' he asked, puzzled. 'Did you spot Rocky coming up to us?'

'No,' admitted Eoin, 'it was these two here who warned me,' pointing to Mick and Brian who had been standing off to one side as the police did their work.

Mick introduced himself to Dylan and Alan.

'I'm glad you are safe now,' he started. 'There's been

more than enough blood spilled in this stadium – and this country – to last us till the end of time.'

CHAPTER 41

The crowd all began to drift away towards the exits, but Eoin, Alan and Dylan hung back to savour the last of a memorable day.

Eoin told Mick how he had seen the shooting on the field below and Brian helping to carry him away.

'I'm sorry you had to see such horrors, young man, but put them from your mind, it was a long time ago.'

Eoin nodded. 'I know, Mick, but I'm sorry you got such a short life because of it.'

'I hadn't a bad one at all,' he replied. 'There were worse than me.'

'Like Perry and Billy,' said Alan.

'Indeed,' replied Mick. 'I meet those youngsters around here all the time. Funny lads, for the most part, always up to mischief.'

Eoin noticed three boys walking down the steps of the stand towards them.

'Here they are,' said Eoin.

'They are indeed, and Jerome O'Leary's with them too. He was shot sitting on the wall at the back of the Canal End.'

'Howya lads,' said Dylan. 'How old are ye all?'

'Well over a hundred,' said Perry, with a grin.

'Ah no, I meant how old were you when, you know…?'

'When we were killed?' asked Billy. 'I was just fourteen.'

'I was ten,' replied Jerome.

'Eleven,' answered Perry. 'I was the first to be shot on Bloody Sunday – I was up a tree trying to get a free look at the game when I heard the armoured cars arrive. I looked around and a bullet caught me in the chest. I lingered for a while, but the doctors couldn't save me.'

'But why?' asked Dylan. 'Why did they shoot you?'

'I don't know, maybe they thought I was signalling to someone inside. I heard one of the soldiers shout 'ambush' but I was only a youngster – I had nothing to do with anything.'

'It was a terrible day all round,' said Mick. 'But it's a long time ago now and the world has turned quite a few times since. Everything has changed – even this place. Would you believe they renamed the stand we're in now after me?' he chuckled.

Two other boys who had been watching the last of the celebrations on the field turned and climbed the steps towards the exit. As they neared the Ormondstown group one of them recognised them.

'Eoin, how are you,' he smiled. 'That was a fantastic game wasn't it? I was just saying to Dan how I hoped we would bump into you.'

'Ah, Michael, it's great to see you,' said Eoin, not sure whether to tell him about the rest of the day's dramas. 'You remember Alan of course, and Dylan's here too.'

'Howya,' said Michael. 'How could I forget Dylan, after he sold us that dummy and punched the ball into our net?'

They all laughed.

'But who are all these other people. I sort of recognise you,' Michael said pointing at the man who carried the same name as him.

Eoin stepped forward and looked Michael in the eye.

'I'm not messing with you here, honestly,' he explained. 'But I have a knack of being able to see ghosts. Sometimes people with me can see them too. These here are all the spirits of those who died here on Bloody Sunday...' he added.

'Great Uncle Michael?' gasped young Michael. 'Is it you?'

The ghost of the Tipperary player looked stunned, but that soon turned to delight as he realised who the two boys from Grangemockler were.

Eoin winked at his friends and made his excuses.

'We have to get our bus now,' he said, 'but I'll leave you three Hogans to catch up. After a hundred years you must have plenty to discuss.'

AUTHOR'S NOTE

Bloody Sunday

Sunday, 21 November 1920, was one of the most tragic and controversial days in Irish history. The War of Independence had been going for almost two years and early on that Sunday morning fourteen British agents and officers were shot dead in their homes by members of the IRA under the command of Michael Collins.

That afternoon, a group of men, made up of soldiers, policemen, Auxiliaries and the 'Black and Tans' – a state paramilitary body who wore a variety of uniforms, hence their nickname – gathered in two locations to the north and south of Croke Park. Inside the ground, Dublin were playing Tipperary in a football challenge match in front of around 5,000 spectators.

The authorities' plan was to seal the ground and to search everyone in attendance, but instead shots were fired at ticket sellers outside and the troops chased them into the ground. Shots continued to be fired for ninety seconds before orders to cease firing were heeded.

Major-General Boyd, officer commanding Dublin District, said: 'the firing on the crowd was carried out without orders, was indiscriminate, and unjustifiable.'

Fourteen men, women and children died of injuries received in Croke Park that day, including three boys – John William 'Billy' Scott (14), William 'Perry' Robinson (11) and Jerome O'Leary (10). The Tipperary corner-back, Mick Hogan, was among those killed.

Further reading: *The Bloodied Field* by Michael Foley (O'Brien Press, 2014)

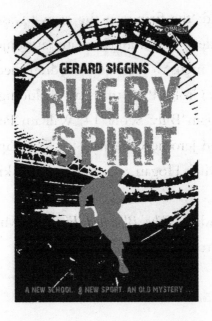

RUGBY SPIRIT

GERARD SIGGINS

RUGBY SPIRIT

A NEW SCHOOL. A NEW SPORT. AN OLD MYSTERY ...

A new school. A new sport. An old mystery...

Eoin's has just started a new school ... and a new sport. Everyone at school is mad about rugby, but Eoin hasn't even held a rugby ball before! And why does everybody seem to know more about his own grandad than he does?

RUGBY WARRIOR

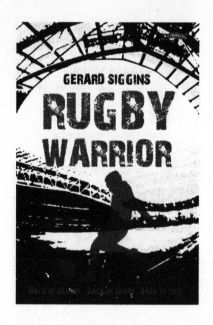

Back in school. Back in sport. Back in time.
Eoin Madden is now captain of the Under 14s team and
has to deal with friction between his friend Rory and
new boy Dylan as they battle for a place as scrum-half.
Fast-paced action, mysterious spirits and feuding friends
– it's a season to remember!

RUGBY REBEL

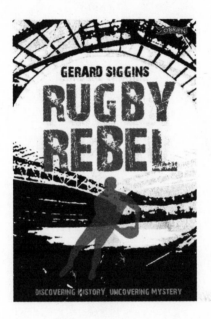

Discovering History. Uncovering Mystery

Eoin Madden's been moved up to train with the Junior Cup team, which is hard work, plus there's trouble in school as mobile phones start going missing! But there are ghostly goings-on in Castlerock – what's the link between Eoin's history lessons and the new spirit he's spotted wearing a Belvedere rugby jersey?

RUGBY FLYER

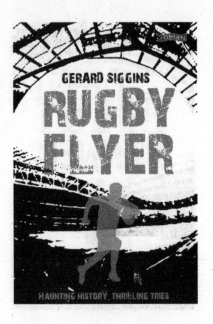

Haunting history. Thrilling tries.

Eoin and his new friends are taken on a trip to Twickenham to play & watch rugby. There, he meets a ghost: Prince Obolensky, a Russian who played rugby for England, scored a world famous try against New Zealand in Twickenham and later joined the RAF and died in WW2.

RUGBY RUNNER

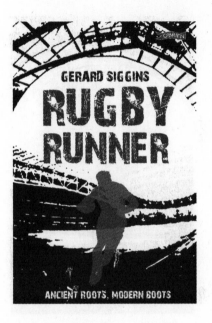

Ancient Roots. Modern boots.

Eoin Madden is captain of the Junior Cup team, training with Leinster and aiming for Ireland's Under 16 World Cup team. He also has to deal with grumpy friends, teachers piling on the homework – AND a ghost on a mission that goes back to the very origins of the game of rugby.

RUGBY HEROES

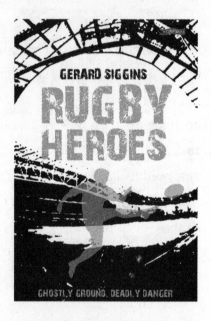

Ghostly Ground, Deadly Danger.

Eoin Madden is Castlerock College's star player and he's been called up for Ireland in the Under 16 Four Nations! When his oldest and best ghostly friend calls for help, can Eoin and his band of heroes solve their deadliest mystery yet?